Louisa, The Heiress in Disguise

A Friends to Lovers Sweet
Historical Romance

Kerri Kastle

Copyright © 2024 by Kerri Kastle

All rights reserved.

No portion of this book may be reproduced in any form without written permission from the publisher or author, except as permitted by U.S. copyright law.

Contents

1. Chapter 1: Louisa — 1
2. Chapter 2: William — 10
3. Chapter 3: Louisa — 19
4. Chapter 4: William — 31
5. Chapter 5: Louisa — 38
6. Chapter 6: William — 52
7. Chapter 7: Louisa — 63
8. Chapter 8: William — 71
9. Chapter 9: Louisa — 79
10. Chapter 10: William — 84
11. Chapter 11: Louisa — 96
12. Chapter 12: William — 107
13. Chapter 13: Louisa — 116
14. Chapter 14: William — 127

15. Chapter 15: Louisa — 134
16. Chapter 16: William — 141
17. Chapter 17: Louisa — 148
18. Chapter 18: William — 155
19. Chapter 19: Louisa — 163
20. Chapter 20: William — 170
21. Chapter 21: Louisa — 179
22. Chapter 22: William — 187
23. Chapter 23: Louisa — 191
24. Chapter 24: William — 199
25. Chapter 25: Louisa — 204

Chapter 1: Louisa

The masquerade ball was a shimmering whirlwind of silk and scandal.

Louisa, dressed in a deep blue gown that disguised her curves more than flattered them, felt like a tiny fish thrust into a tank of piranhas. Every jeweled garment and painted smile felt like a silent accusation.

Her aunt Beatrice, a woman whose smile could curdle milk, had practically shoved her into the carriage, all but shrieking about the importance of "making a good impression" on Lord Thorne.

Louisa knew better.

Lord Thorne, with his extreme flattery and gaze that lingered too long on young girls, sent shivers running down her spine. He was bad news, and Louisa, bless her rebellious heart, had no intention of becoming his latest conquest.

Avoiding a lively dance, Louisa looked around the ballroom for her younger sister, Hannah.

Hannah, unlike Louisa, was all soft smiles and naive optimism. Louisa feared Beatrice had also set her sights on Hannah for Thorne's devilish use or any other withering old man.

That's exactly why she was here. No one was to touch her innocent sister, even if it meant giving herself away or putting herself in trouble.

Low murmurs of conversation, laced with amusement, drifted past her ear.

Two young gentlemen, their classy attire clashing with their scorning words, were saying, "Thorne and the Hastings chit, hm? Seems a bit hasty, wouldn't you say?"

"Beatrice Hastings is desperate. The girl is on the shelf, and Thorne needs a hefty dowry. Money over love, the usual tragedy."

Louisa's hand clenched into a fist. Disgust curdled in her stomach.

A marriage built on desperation and money.

Absolutely not.

She wouldn't be a pawn in their game.

Suddenly, a wave of dizziness washed over her. Panic clawed at her throat.

The suffocating heat, the endless press of bodies ... it was all too much.

She needed air and to quickly tell her aunt what she had just heard.

Louisa pushed her way through the crowd, desperate for the cool night beyond the French doors.

Just as she reached the balcony, a figure materialized from the shadows and she bumped him softly, gazing as she took a quick step back.

Tall, broad-shouldered, and clad in a midnight-blue mask that hid the upper half of his face, the man seemed to have appeared out of nowhere.

He was undeniably handsome, his strong jawline hinting at a stubborn streak, and his dark eyes, although obscured by the mask, seemed to pierce right through her.

"Whoa there, little runaway," he drawled, his voice a low rumble that sent a shiver down her spine. He wasn't crude, but his amusement was clear.

Before Louisa could muster a reply, a strong hand clamped around her wrist, sending an electric jolt through her arm. He didn't ask permission. He simply steered her back towards the dance floor.

"Ah the waltz, great for conversation," he stated, his voice surprisingly gentle.

Louisa, her temper flaring, yanked her arm back. "I have no intention of conversing with a stranger, let alone waltzing with one!"

His lips twitched, a hint of a smile threatening to break through. "Intriguing. Most ladies at a ball are quite eager for conversation, especially with a handsome stranger."

"Most ladies," she retorted, her voice laced with ice, "lack the spine to refuse a dance."

He raised an eyebrow, amusement reflecting in his eyes. "Ah, a woman with a backbone. That's even more intriguing." Before she could protest further, he swept her into the large crowd of dancers.

The audacity of the man! Louisa bristled, her body pressed against his as they began to waltz.

Yet, despite her anger, a strange warmth spread within her. This wasn't the suffocating pressure she felt with Thorne.

This stranger, with his masked face and teasing demeanor, was... different.

Louisa fumed as they glided across the polished floor.

His hand, surprisingly warm and calloused, rested firmly on her waist, guiding her steps.

This stranger danced with a confident grace, his movements mirroring hers with a practiced ease.

"You waltz remarkably well for someone so averse to conversation," he remarked, his voice a low murmur that tickled her ear.

Louisa arched an eyebrow. "Perhaps some ladies enjoy conversation, but this lady prefers competent dance partners."

A low chuckle rumbled in his chest, sending a shiver down her spine despite her best efforts to resist it. "Competency, then? A high bar, Miss...?"

"Hastings," she supplied, her voice clipped.

"Miss Hastings," he repeated, savoring the name on his tongue. "A pleasure. Though I must confess, I expected a warmer welcome from such a captivating creature."

Louisa scoffed. "Flattery will get you nowhere, sir. Especially when delivered by a masked stranger."

"Ah, but that's the beauty of the mask, isn't it?" he countered, his voice taking on a teasing lilt. "It allows for a touch of honesty without the burden of social niceties."

"Honesty?" Louisa challenged, her gaze locking with his through the narrow eye holes of his mask. "Is that what you call waltzing with a woman against her will?"

He raised his hand in mock surrender. "A slight exaggeration, wouldn't you say? You seemed quite eager to escape the clutches of boredom, judging by your hasty retreat to the balcony."

Louisa couldn't deny the truth in his statement. The stifling atmosphere of the ballroom, coupled with the news of her impending marriage, had left her desperate for a breath of fresh air.

Yet, she wouldn't give this infuriating man the satisfaction of admitting it.

"Boredom," she sniffed, "is a far cry from the suffocating pressure one encounters while dancing with the wrong gentleman."

He studied her for a moment, his masked gaze seeming to pierce right through her. "And who, pray tell, constitutes the 'wrong gentleman'?"

Hesitantly, Louisa glanced around the room. Aunt Beatrice, her predatory smile plastered on her face, stood conversing with a group of ladies, and in their midst, Lord Thorne stood. "There," she murmured, gesturing discreetly with her chin. "Lord Thorne."

His brow furrowed, and for the first time, a flicker of something akin to anger crossed his masked face. "Thorne," he repeated, the name a low growl. "That oily-haired peacock? What has he done to earn your disdain?"

Louisa hesitated.

Sharing the details of her predicament with a stranger felt reckless, yet there was something about this man, something in the way he held himself, that commanded a hesitant trust.

"He's the gentleman," she began, her voice barely a whisper, "my Aunt Beatrice has chosen for me."

No spark flickered in his eyes, almost as if he wasn't surprised. "An arranged marriage, then?"

Louisa nodded, a lump forming in her throat. "A loveless transaction. You don't seem surprised."

"You could say I already knew about that, Miss Hastings. It's the main gossip of tonight. I could bet all I have that everyone in this ballroom knows."

Louisa sighed, fighting a hard urge to roll her eyes.

His hand tightened around her waist, a silent gesture of support amidst the whirling chaos of the dance floor. "Well," he murmured, his voice low and intense, "consider this: you won't be waltzing with Lord Thorne tonight."

A flicker of something she couldn't quite define ignited within her.

This stranger, with his masked face and teasing self, had somehow managed to spark a rebellious fire within her.

"And who," she challenged, meeting his gaze head-on, "decides who I waltz with?"

He leaned closer, his lips brushing her ear.

The warmth of his breath sent goosebumps erupting across her skin. "Perhaps," he whispered, a hint of a smile playing on his lips, "tonight, we both do."

The music swelled to a crescendo, and they continued to dance, a silent battle of wills playing out beneath the shimmering chandeliers.

Louisa, for the first time all night, felt a strange sense of exhilaration.

As they twirled across the polished floor, Louisa allowed herself a stolen moment of carefree joy.

The stranger, with his confident hand guiding her and his playfully teasing words, was a welcome distraction from the suffocating reality.

But the ballroom, with its swirling silks and glittering chandeliers, was a treacherous place.

A glance towards the balcony, where she'd momentarily sought refuge, served as a stark reminder. Aunt Beatrice, her smile devoid of warmth, was deep in conversation with a man whose face she couldn't see.

With a growing sense of unease, Louisa searched for her sister.

Relief washed over her as she spotted Hannah gliding across the floor with a young gentleman, her face lit with a genuine smile.

That was Hannah, ever the optimist, blissfully unaware of the machinations swirling around them.

But her moment of relief was short-lived. Her gaze darted back to the balcony, and a cold dread settled in her stomach.

The man had turned around, revealing the oily smirk of Lord Thorne.

Louisa's blood ran cold.

The overheard conversation, Beatrice's desperate attempts to "make a good impression," and now this. It all clicked into a horrifying place.

Beatrice wasn't interested in securing a good marriage for Louisa; she was interested in securing her hefty dowry.

Disgust churned in her stomach.

Her aunt, the woman who should have been her protector, was willing to sacrifice her happiness for a bit of financial security.

The anger simmering within her threatened to boil over.

Suddenly, the stranger's hand tightened around her waist, subtly pulling her closer. "Something troubles you," he said, his voice low and concerned.

Louisa glanced sideways, her voice chilly. "Let's just say I've stumbled upon a rather unpleasant truth."

He raised an eyebrow, a silent invitation for her to elaborate, and a surge of panic flooded Louisa's veins.

Why was he so interested in this?

Then a wave of suspicion washed over her.

What did he know of her situation? Was he somehow involved in Beatrice's scheme?

"Forgive me," she blurted out, her voice betraying her growing unease. "I misspoke. This... unpleasant truth is nothing of your concern."

The final notes of the waltz faded into the background, and Louisa, seizing the opportunity, offered a curt nod to her masked partner. "Thank you for the dance, sir, but I require fresh air."

Without waiting for a response, she swept away from him, her heart pounding a frantic tattoo against her ribs.

The ballroom floor seemed to tilt beneath her feet, the shimmering gowns and swirling couples blurring into a dizzying spectacle.

She needed to escape, to clear her head and formulate a plan.

Emerging from the heavy oak doors, Louisa stumbled into the cool night air.

The vast expanse of the Harriet estate stretched before her, bathed in the soft glow of the moon. The rustling of leaves in the nearby gardens provided the only sound to her churning thoughts.

Beatrice was plotting to sell her off like a prized mare at auction.

And the worst part? Louisa couldn't simply refuse.

Doing so would not only disgrace her family, but also put Hannah in a precarious position.

Aunt Beatrice, desperate for the financial security a marriage with Thorne would provide, wouldn't hesitate to turn her cruel gaze towards Hannah if Louisa wasn't 'compliant.'

Frustration gnawed at her.

Louisa was not a pawn to be manipulated by a greedy aunt and a lecherous suitor.

She was Louisa Hastings, a woman of spirit and intellect, and she wouldn't go down without a fight.

But what fight?

Her options seemed as suffocating as the ballroom she'd just escaped.

Running away wasn't an option. Society would ostracize her, leaving her destitute and alone. And elopement with someone... anyone... was simply out of the question.

Their society wouldn't tolerate such a scandal, and besides, who in their right mind would want to run away with a woman facing financial ruin and a vengeful aunt?

"Louisa." Aunt Beatrice's voice cut through the darkness, her shrill tone laced with irritation.

Louisa turned towards the open French doors of the ballroom, her blood running cold at the sight that greeted her.

Beatrice stood there, her arm linked with Lord Thorne's, a sickeningly smug expression plastered on her face.

Beside them stood Hannah, her usual joyous smile replaced by a look of bewildered concern. Her dance partner, a tall man with an air of aristocracy about him, stood awkwardly to the side.

He looked every bit the part of a duke or earl, his elegant attire and confident posture a stark contrast to Lord Thorne's oily demeanor.

Louisa's mind raced.

Had Aunt Beatrice already informed Thorne of their 'arrangement'? Or was Hannah simply worried about her hasty escape? The uncertainty gnawed at her.

Regardless, Louisa knew she couldn't hide. Her aunt, with relentless pursuit of propriety, would surely drag her back inside. Taking a deep breath, she squared her shoulders and walked towards them, the moon casting long shadows as she stepped out of the darkness.

You can do this, Louisa!

She thought to herself as she walked.

Can I?

Chapter 2: William

An hour earlier...

Goodness, William thought. *I'd give anything to escape the disaster of this... royal masked ball tonight.*

A plume of dust howled softly behind the luxurious golden carriage as it rolled to a halt on the gravel driveway.

William, the Earl of Blackwood, came out first, his posture stiff and his expression a stormy cloud.

The brisk autumn wind whipped at his dark hair, mirroring the annoyance brewing within him.

The grand royal estate, seated atop a rolling hill, sprawled before them.

Towers adorned with gargoyles clawed at the dark sky, and flickering torches cast moving shadows across the ivy-covered stone walls.

The air hummed with quiet, soft activity known to cater to the rich—the type he disliked the most.

It's time to leave London, he thought. *I can't take another of these frustrating gatherings for gossip.*

Servants ran around to help people, carriages lined the drive, and laughter and soft music drifted from the open windows of the castle.

But William felt no joy in the festivities. He never did.

Tonight's grand masked ball was an unwelcome interruption to his research on ancient civilizations, a duty forced upon him by his ever-so-socially-conscious mother.

"William darling, for goodness' sake, straighten your dark bow and adjust that scowl. I really think you should have worn a brighter color for your bow," said the Dowager Countess Blackwood, a beautiful, stern-looking woman draped in shimmering emerald silks. Her perfectly coiffed hair and bright eyes made her look younger than her advanced age. "Now you look unapproachable."

William grunted, a silent rebellion against the societal pressures she constantly heaped upon him. "Approachable to whom, Mother? A sea of debutantes only interested in my title and nothing else?"

The dowager countess huffed. "Dear son, you are the Earl of Blackwood. It is your duty to perpetuate the lineage. These debutantes are important in your life. You know this ... especially after what happened."

His mother, Lady Beth, immediately realized she had said something wrong as soon as the words left her lips and she winced.

William just stared at her with dark, emotionless eyes.

"Titles help secure long-lasting alliances, son," she said in a softer voice. "Besides, wouldn't a young lady bring a touch of light and life to our gloomy castle?"

He scoffed. "Light? Life? My home has had enough of both, Mother. Ghosts from those lights and life still whisper through the halls. I'm not willing to go through that again."

Was the death of his beloved wife going to be forgotten so soon?

If everyone else forgot, he didn't think he would ever forget it. The memory of it haunted him every second.

It had been years, but it still felt like it happened yesterday.

A pained look flickered across the dowager countess' face, quickly masked by her usual steely resolve.

William knew his words cut deep, for his mother also had loved Anna, whose death had taken a toll on her.

But no matter. The aristocracy valued tradition over feelings, and tonight was all about upholding tradition.

And lineage, apparently.

As they started their ascent towards the castle's imposing double doors, another cloud of dust signaled the arrival of another carriage.

William glanced sideways, a flicker of curiosity sparking in his dark eyes. This carriage wasn't as luxurious as his, its sleek, polished, dark wood standing apart from the flashy opulence of others.

A young woman emerged, her movements surprisingly swift for someone clad in a gown of blue silk. She held her head high, the golden mask on her face doing nothing to hide the annoyance etched across her features, mirroring his own sentiment perfectly.

His brows went up. Did she also not want to be here? What lady was not excited about the thought of a masked ball?

This lady, it seemed.

Her hair, a cascade of auburn fire, danced in the wind, momentarily blinding him with its vibrancy.

He could only catch glimpses of her face as she turned away—a sharp jawline, a strong nose, and eyes the color of twilight—before her chaperone, a stout woman with a too-tight bun, hurried to her side.

"Louisa, you must remember your manners tonight," the woman hissed, her voice sharp enough to cut through the din. "Lord Thorne is here, and this is your chance to make a good impression! You know he's the perfect suitor for you!"

Louisa, as William presumed her to be, merely rolled her eyes.

Her defiance was refreshing, a stark contrast to the fake smiles he usually encountered at such social gatherings.

A smirk tugged at the corner of his mouth—perhaps this ball wouldn't be entirely devoid of amusement after all.

"Don't worry, Aunt," Louisa drawled sarcastically, her voice a low husky tone, sending a strange sensation through me.

She turned to help another woman out of the carriage, whispering to her. "Lord Thorne won't know what hit him. I plan to have him running for the hills soon."

The lady giggled. "Honestly, sister," the younger lady muttered, "I think Lord Thorne is a good man and you should open your heart to him."

William raised an eyebrow. Lord Thorne, that notorious gentleman?

Louisa scoffed. "And you are too naïve, my darling sister. Must you fuss over me so? It's not like anyone here is worth the effort."

"You're a good woman, sister. You need a husband, and lord Thorne has a charming smile."

"Lord Thorne wouldn't know a good woman if she tripped over him and landed in his lap, Hannah," she retorted. "Besides, have you seen the man's mustache? It's positively disastrous!"

A strange warmth bloomed in his chest. Here was a woman who didn't seem fazed by an impressive title ... or anything else for that matter. Could she be the one to break through his self-imposed isolation and bring some light into his life, as his mother so desired? Or was she just another beautiful face hiding a cunning heart, as cynical William suspected?

Tonight, William decided he would observe.

Crystal chandeliers cast a shimmering glow over the royal estate's splendid ballroom.

The air thrummed with a symphony of string music, chattering debutantes, and the rhythmic thud of feet against the polished marble floor.

William felt out of place. This wasn't his type of crowd.

His mother, who decided to make his life hell for the night, leaned closer. "William, darling," she cooed, her voice barely audible over the din. "There's Lady Ashton, a delightful girl, quite accomplished on the pianoforte. Go have a chat with her, why don't you?"

William mumbled a polite no, his eyes sweeping the room with practiced indifference.

He had seen this dance a hundred times before—mothers angling, daughters fluttering their eyelashes, all in the grand game of securing a wealthy husband. It was a dance he had no interest in participating in.

Lady Blackwood, her smile a touch strained, moved on to another potential candidate. "And there's Miss Davies." She pointed towards a young woman with hair like spun gold. "Her family owns half of Yorkshire. A very good match, wouldn't you say?"

William offered another curt dismissal.

His mother, her patience wearing thin, finally fixed him with a steely gaze. "Son," she hissed, her voice low and stressed, "you are here to choose a bride, remember? Not to scowl at the wall like it took your candy!"

Out of the corner of his eye, William caught sight of the woman with the emerald eyes and the unfortunate mustache commentary. Lady Louisa, if he recalled correctly.

She was looking just as out of place as he did. She looked around, eyes wide with what looked like nerves.

He tilted his head to the side as he watched her, wondering what had happened to her.

She was surrounded by a group of giggling girls, their diamond tiaras winking under the warm light.

An idea, sparked by a glint of rebellious amusement, flickered in William's mind. "Very well, Mother," he said, his voice surprisingly calm. "I shall dance."

His mother beamed, her earlier frustration melting away. "Excellent! Now, who shall it be?"

Without a word, William stalked across the ballroom floor, his boots clicking on the polished marble. As he passed the doors leading to the balcony, Lady Louisa ran right into him. His hands immediately held her right before he pulled away, ignoring the startled gasps of the surrounding girls.

A little gasp left her lips as she looked up at him. Her gold mask was so beautiful, and it made her skin look ethereal. It also made her lips look enticing.

He cleared his throat. "Whoa there, little runaway."

She scowled at him, and he grinned.

Ah, exactly what he needed.

Or so he thought.

***

William left the ball even more confused than when he entered.

The carriage rattled along the moonlit path as they rode back home, the ball successfully ended.

William stared out the window, his mind replaying the events of the evening. Lady Louisa had been a refreshing change from the usual soulless chit-chat of debutantes. She had fire, she wasn't afraid to speak, and that made him curious.

Their dance had been a polite waltz, their bodies barely touching. But even with that, there had been a spark in her dark gaze, a challenge that had intrigued him. Apart from the spark, he also saw a shadow lurking in her eyes, a flicker of something he couldn't quite understand.

He recalled the way she had ended their dance: abruptly excusing herself and running away.

As they danced, the color had suddenly drained from her face, and her hand trembled slightly when she touched his.

What had really happened to her?

He wanted to know, but he hadn't seen her again. And he didn't even know what she looked like without her mask.

William frowned.

Apart from Lady Louisa, the entire evening had been a charade orchestrated by his mother.

He was tired of being pushed towards societal expectations, tired of the suffocating feeling of obligation.

Marriage wasn't a game; it was a sacred union, and he refused to enter into it to make his mother happy, or to secure an heir.

As the carriage rolled out through the grand gates of Blackwood Manor, a resolution formed. He wouldn't play their game anymore.

They entered a large, dimly lit drawing room where Lady Blackwood awaited, her face lined with anticipation. William nodded, dismissing the footman who helped him out of his coat, and approached his mother.

"Well, William?" she inquired, her voice laced with nervous excitement. "Have you chosen a ... suitable candidate? You danced quite beautifully with Lady Louisa tonight."

"Did I?"

"You two looked so good together. Will you marry her?"

He met her gaze with a steely resolve. "Mother," he said, his voice calm but firm, "I have decided I will not marry any of the ladies I met tonight."

Lady Blackwood's smile faltered. "William darling, you need an heir!" she protested. "The Blackwood lineage cannot end with you." His mother was starting to get hysterical.

"There will be an heir, Mother," he assured her, his voice firm. "But it will be on my terms and not dictated by anyone else. Not you, not society."

A wave of disappointment washed over Lady Blackwood's face. "But William," she pleaded, "you haven't met anyone since ... since Anna."

The mention of his late wife brought a pang of sorrow to William's heart. Anna, with her gentle spirit and boundless love for life, had left a void in his heart and a sadness no one deserved.

"I haven't, and I don't intend to," he said, his voice hardening. "Love is not a commodity to be bartered in a ballroom. I will find a wife when the time is right ... when I meet someone who stirs my soul like Anna did."

Lady Blackwood sighed, her shoulders slumping in defeat. "Son, you cannot simply abandon your responsibilities! What will people say?"

"Let them gossip," William retorted, his voice laced with a bitterness he couldn't quite shake no matter how hard he tried. "I will not sacrifice my happiness on the altar of social approval."

He knew his words would have consequences, but frankly, he didn't care.

He craved peace, a chance to escape the suffocating expectations of aristocracy.

He had a small estate in a neighboring town, a quiet haven where he could lose himself in his books and the solace of solitude.

"I am leaving for the second Blackwood Manor tomorrow, Mother," he announced. "I will find a suitable wife in my own time, a woman who values intellect and companionship, not titles and wealth."

Seeing the resolve in his eyes, Lady Blackwood knew further arguments were futile. With a defeated sigh, she nodded her consent. "Very well, William," she said. "Go. But promise me you will find someone … someone who will bring joy back into your life."

William squeezed her hand gently. "I promise, Mother. I will find someone worthy of the Blackwood name."

Later that night, William bid farewell to his mother and entered his carriage, journeying back to his quiet estate. As he rumbled away from the imposing walls of Blackwood Manor, he felt a sense of liberation.

He didn't know when or where he would find her, this woman who would hold the key to his heart, but he had a newfound determination, a flicker of hope that somewhere there existed a soul that matched his own. And when he did find her, he wouldn't let her go.

Chapter 3: Louisa

The ride home was a blur.

Louisa forced a smile onto her lips as Aunt Beatrice prattled on about Lord Thorne's "charm and wit." Hannah, silent and watchful beside her, cast Louisa worried glances.

All evening, Lord Thorne's oily gaze had lingered on Louisa in a way that made her skin crawl, along with his steady stream of empty compliments.

Inside the mansion, the oppressive atmosphere thickened.

The servants, usually bustling with quiet efficiency, seemed to hold their breath as Aunt Beatrice ushered them all into the drawing room.

The heavy oak doors closed behind them with a finality that sent shivers down Louisa's spine.

Louisa sighed hard as she walked in. She had suffered a lot of shivers down her spine today, and it was wearing on her.

When Lord Thorne arrived at the mansion soon after, Aunt Beatrice, her predatory smile never faltering, suggested Hannah join her for a cup of tea.

Louisa was left alone, a lone pawn in a game she desperately wanted to overturn.

Her mind raced.

Aunt Beatrice's plan was becoming terrifyingly clear. She'd isolate Louisa, leaving her vulnerable to Lord Thorne's advances.

The very thought of it sent a wave of nausea coursing through her.

But Louisa, bless her rebellious heart, wouldn't go down without a fight.

She scanned the room, searching for an escape or a weapon, anything to disrupt her aunt's scheme.

"Louisa," Aunt Beatrice called, her voice dripping with a feigned sweetness. "Lord Thorne was just expressing his admiration for your spirited waltz."

Lord Thorne, his oily smile widening at Louisa's name, gave a theatrical bow. "Indeed, Miss Hastings. A most delightful dance."

Louisa almost grimaced but she held it back. She had hated the forced dance with Lord Thorne.

It disgusted her more every second she recalled it.

"The pleasure was mine, Lord Thorne." Louisa offered a curt nod, insincerity dripping from her lips.

A flicker of annoyance crossed her aunt's face, barely concealed by the smile plastered on her lips. "Well then, perhaps you can offer Lord Thorne some refreshments in the drawing room. I'm certain he'd appreciate your company."

The implication was clear.

Beatrice wanted Louisa alone with Thorne, a classic ploy to create a 'compromising' situation. Louisa gritted her teeth, her anger simmering just beneath the surface.

"I'm afraid I must decline, Aunt," Louisa said, her voice firm. "I'm feeling a bit fatigued and require some solitude in my chambers."

Disbelief flickered across Aunt Beatrice's face, quickly replaced by a forced smile. "Nonsense, Louisa. Surely a bit of conversation won't hurt."

Louisa held her aunt's gaze, her resolve hardening. "I don't think I can, Aunt. I feel so dizzy I could faint now. If you'll excuse me."

With a defiant tilt of her chin, Louisa swept past them, her silk skirts whispering against the polished marble floor.

The tension in the air was thick enough to cut with a knife.

Reaching the sanctuary of her room, Louisa slammed the door shut with a resounding thud. The sound echoed through the room, a physical manifestation of the frustration roiling within her. She paced the room, the elegant furniture becoming obstacles in her agitated state.

Suddenly, a soft knock on the door startled her.

"Louisa, may I come in?" It was Hannah's voice, laced with a hint of trepidation.

Louisa took a deep breath, willing her anger to subside. "Come in, Hannah," she called out.

The door creaked open, revealing a worried Hannah. Relief washed over Louisa, momentarily calming the storm within her.

"Louisa," Hannah began, her voice barely above a whisper, "I know something's wrong. Don't pretend there's not."

Louisa sighed, collapsing onto the plush chaise lounge. "There's too much to explain, Hannah."

"Try me," Hannah persisted, her voice surprisingly resolute.

Hesitantly, Louisa recounted the overheard whispers and, most importantly, their Aunt's scheme to marry her off to Lord Thorne. Hannah listened intently, her face betraying a range of emotions—fear, anger, and finally, a steely resolve.

"Louisa ... I know," she began, "I know what Aunt has been up to."

Relief flooded Louisa's chest. She wasn't alone in her suspicions. "You do?"

Hannah nodded. "I overheard Aunt talking with Lord Thorne. She wants you to be ... compromised tonight."

Louisa felt a cold dread settle in her stomach.

"This is awful, Louisa," Hannah finally said, her voice tight with anger. "I know you want to get away and the only thing stopping you is me. But you don't have to worry. I'll be ok."

Louisa raised an eyebrow, skepticism etched on her face. "What do you mean you'll be ok?"

A sweet, sly smile spread across Hannah's face. "Remember Duke Dan, the gentleman I was dancing with?"

Louisa nodded, a flicker of curiosity sparking in her eyes.

"Well," Hannah said, "he seems quite smitten."

"Smitten?" Louisa echoed, a disbelieving laugh escaping her lips.

"Absolutely," Hannah insisted. "He practically confessed his undying devotion while we were dancing. And you know what else? He's a duke. He's wealthy!"

Louisa's skepticism began to waver.

Yes! That is true!

If Duke is in love with Hannah, and he is rich, that means she will be married to him soon.

"Hannah..." Louisa began, unsure how to articulate the jumble of emotions swirling within her.

"Trust me, Louisa," Hannah interrupted, her voice filled with a newfound confidence. "Duke Dan will take care of everything. Aunt Beatrice won't dare object to a duke, especially one with such a substantial fortune. So, you don't have to worry about me. Do what you must. I know you love your freedom."

A flicker of hope ignited within Louisa. Could it be this simple?

Could Hannah, with her naive charm and unexpected dance partner, be the key to her liberation?

Despite the lingering doubts, a sense of calm settled over Louisa. For the first time that night, she allowed herself to believe in the possibility of a happy ending.

But even so, she was still very skeptical.

"But Hannah ..."

"No, Louisa. No buts! You can't let Aunt Beatrice do this to you. You must get away before she ties you down forever. It would break my heart to see that happen."

Despite the glimmer of hope flickering within her, a pang of guilt jabbed at Louisa's heart.

Hannah, ever selfless, was willing to face their fearsome aunt alone so Louisa could escape. The thought of leaving her younger sister behind was unbearable.

"Hannah," Louisa began, her voice thick with emotion, "are you sure about this? I can't ask you to face Aunt Beatrice's wrath on your own."

Hannah, her chin held high in a show of defiance, met Louisa's gaze. "Nonsense, Louisa. You know me. I've always been the better negotiator." A hint of mischief danced in her eyes. "Besides, with Duke Dan smitten and Aunt Beatrice desperate for a wealthy suitor, I think I can manage."

Louisa couldn't help but smile at Hannah's naiveté.

While charming, Duke Dan might not be the solution Hannah believed him to be.

Yet, there was a newfound resolve in Hannah's voice, a strength Louisa hadn't before seen. Perhaps, Louisa thought, Hannah wouldn't need rescuing after all.

"Perhaps you're right," Louisa conceded, a hint of amusement softening her voice. "Just promise me you'll be careful."

"Of course," Hannah chirped, her usual cheerfulness returning. "Now, come on. We need to get you out of here before the first rooster crows."

Leaving?

Tonight?

The thought sent a jolt through Louisa. Leaving everything behind, the familiar comfort of the Hasting estate, the life she knew, seemed reckless, yet oddly liberating.

Hannah, sensing her apprehension, reached out and squeezed her hand. "Don't worry, Louisa. I have a plan. You can go to Mary."

Mary.

The name brought a flicker of warmth to Louisa's heart.

Mary, their former governess, had been like a second mother to them. Kind, resourceful, and fiercely loyal, Mary had instilled in both sisters a love for learning and a rebellious streak that often landed them in trouble.

"Mary?" Louisa repeated, a ghost of a smile playing on her lips.

"Of course," Hannah beamed. "She'll take you in. I know it. Besides, wouldn't you love to see her quaint little cottage again?"

A wave of nostalgia washed over Louisa. Memories of lazy summer afternoons spent reading in Mary's cozy cottage garden, her warm laughter and endless supply of stories, all flooded back.

The idea of reconnecting with Mary offered a comforting sense of familiarity amidst the whirlwind of emotions.

"Yes," Louisa admitted, a genuine smile finally breaking through. "I would love to see Mary again."

With a shared glance, a silent acknowledgment of the life-altering decision Louisa was about to make, they tiptoed down the creaking stairs.

Their loyal maid, Clara, showed up like an angel, a small satchel filled with essentials clutched in her hand. Her knowing smile and a silent squeeze of Louisa's hand spoke volumes.

The vast Hasting estate slept soundly under the cloak of night. Louisa, her heart thundering in her chest, tiptoed out into the cool night air, the silence broken only by the chirping of crickets and the rustle of leaves.

Another shiver danced down Louisa's spine, this one a mixture of fear and excitement. She was leaving everything behind—the familiar comfort of the estate, the stifling life she'd known. Uncertainty gnawed at her, but it was overshadowed by a fierce determination to forge her own path, a path free from Aunt Beatrice's control and a loveless marriage.

Reaching the carriage house, Clara helped Louisa climb into a waiting carriage to which a sturdy horse was hitched. This faithful mare, Clara's secret provision, was her ticket to freedom. With a final glance at the imposing silhouette of the mansion, Louisa turned to Hannah, who stood a few paces away.

The moonlight cast long shadows on Hannah's face, highlighting the worry etched beneath the bravado. Yet, there was also a look of pride in her eyes, a silent acknowledgment of Louisa's courage.

"Take care of yourself, Hannah," Louisa said. "And for goodness' sake, don't let Aunt Beatrice bully you."

Hannah walked towards the carriage, a mischievous glint in her eyes. "Don't worry about me, Louisa. You just worry about enjoying your freedom. And write as soon as you reach Mary's!"

Louisa leaned forward, engulfing Hannah in a tight embrace. For a moment, the weight of their situation pressed down on them. But as they pulled apart, a sense of determination settled on Louisa's shoulders.

"I will," Louisa promised, her voice firm. "And thank you, Hannah. For everything."

Tears welled up in Louisa's eyes. Never had Hannah expressed such wisdom, such a deep understanding of Louisa's yearning for independence.

"Promise me," Louisa whispered, her voice thick with emotion, "you'll write to me. Tell me everything."

"Every detail," Hannah vowed, a playful glint returning to her eyes. "And when I become Duchess Dan," she added with a wink, "you'll come to visit me in a grand castle, and we'll have endless cups of tea and gossip just like we used to."

A choked laugh escaped Louisa's lips. The image of a mischievous Duchess Hannah, regaling her with tales of her opulent life, was a source of unexpected comfort.

Clara cleared her throat, a subtle reminder of the ticking clock.

"Take care of yourself, Hannah," Louisa murmured.

"And you too, Louisa," Hannah replied, her voice trembling slightly. "Go live your life, and don't you ever look back unless it's to appreciate how far you've come."

Without another word, Clara flicked the reins, and the carriage lurched forward, carrying Louisa away from the opulent prison that was her home and towards an uncertain future.

As the carriage rolled away, Louisa stole one last glance at the imposing silhouette of Hasting Manor. It was a goodbye to a gilded cage, but also a farewell to a part of herself, the carefree girl who had once called this place home.

The sounds of the horses' hooves against the ground provided a steady counterpoint to the storm of emotions churning within Louisa.

Fear, yes, for the unknown path ahead. But also, a fierce optimism. She was free.

Free from Aunt Beatrice's manipulations. Free to find her own happiness.

A single tear escaped her eye.

The journey ahead was shrouded in mystery, but Louisa, for the first time in a long time, felt a flicker of hope.

The rhythmic clatter of the carriage wheels gradually lulled Louisa into a fitful sleep.

She dreamt of sprawling meadows, a quaint cottage nestled amidst wildflowers, and Mary's warm smile.

But the peace was suddenly shattered by the jarring halt of the carriage. Her eyes snapped open to find Clara gripping the reins, fear etched on her face.

"What is it?" Louisa demanded, a knot forming in her stomach.

"Miss Louisa, riders are approaching from behind," Clara stammered. "They bear the Manor crest."

Thorne's men!

Louisa's blood ran cold.

Aunt Beatrice must have discovered her escape and sent a search party.

Panic threatened to consume her, but she forced it down, her father's voice echoing in her memory, "A Hasting woman never crumbles under pressure."

Thinking fast, Louisa instructed Clara to take a detour, leading them onto a barely-there track that snaked through a dense forest.

The carriage lurched and swayed as it bounced over uneven terrain, branches of towering oaks scraping the roof.

The sound of the approaching riders grew fainter till it faded away entirely.

Relief washed over Louisa, but it was short-lived. The forest path, barely visible even in the fading moonlight, soon petered out into a tangled undergrowth.

Clara, with a grimace, brought the carriage to a halt.

"We can't go further, Miss Louisa," she declared, her voice strained. "The horses won't be able to manage this."

Louisa understood.

Sleep seemed like a distant memory, replaced by a gnawing anxiety. They huddled together in the cramped carriage, the silence broken only by the chirping of crickets and the rustling of leaves in the wind.

As dawn painted the horizon with streaks of gold and pink, Louisa knew they couldn't stay put. Aunt Beatrice's men would be relentless, and sooner or later, they'd find them.

"Clara," Louisa said, her voice firm despite the tremor running through her, "I will get out of here on foot. Take the carriage back to Hastings Manor. Tell them you lost sight of me."

Clara's jaw clenched. "But Miss Louisa, what about you? It's not safe out here alone."

"I'll be alright," Louisa lied, a steely resolve hardening her features. "There's a small town a few miles north from here—a quaint place with kind people. Mary used to tell us stories about it."

Mary's cottage was out of the question. Aunt Beatrice, in her desperation, would surely have sent men there first.

This small town, this unknown entity, was a gamble, but it was their only chance.

Clara reluctantly agreed. After an emotional goodbye, Louisa watched as the carriage disappeared down the forest path, a lone teardrop rolling down her cheek.

Alone, Louisa squared her shoulders and set off in the direction Mary had indicated would lead to the place.

The sun, now fully risen, beat down mercilessly, but the thick forest offered some shade. Her once elegant gown, now snagged by thorns and dusted with dirt, felt suffocating. But Louisa pressed on, fueled by a burning desire for freedom and a deep-seated fear of what awaited her if she was caught.

Hours passed in a blur of exhaustion and hunger. Doubt began to gnaw at her.

Had Mary been mistaken about the town? Was she hopelessly lost?

Just as despair threatened to engulf her, Louisa saw a sign right in the middle of the woods.

An inn. For weary travelers.

Oh, thank goodness! She thought and started to trudge listlessly toward the small building.

She just hoped it wasn't some type of trap designed to lure innocent travelers like herself ... because at that point, she didn't care. She just needed a roof over her head so she could rest.

With renewed strength, Louisa quickened her steps, her tattered gown billowing behind her.

She entered the inn, its sign proclaiming it "The Traveler's Rest."

It looked like heaven to her.

The warm glow of the hearth beckoned her in. Inside, a cheerful innkeeper, a stout woman named Martha, greeted her with a kind smile.

If the woman was that nice, the inn had to be a good place.

Louisa, her voice hoarse from thirst and exhaustion, managed to ask for a room and some food.

Martha, sensing her distress, ushered her into a cozy corner booth and poured her a steaming cup of tea.

As Louisa devoured a plate of warm bread and cheese, Martha listened intently to her fabricated story.

Louisa claimed to be a traveling governess who had become separated from her employer during a journey.

Though Martha's eyes held a hint of suspicion, she offered Louisa a sympathetic smile and a room for the night.

Exhaustion finally overtook Louisa.

She collapsed onto the surprisingly comfortable bed, the worn linen sheets a welcome respite from the harsh forest floor.

The next day, it was after she had thanked Martha, gone ahead on her journey, and walked far from the inn that she realized she had been robbed of all her coins.

She was heartbroken and contemplated going back, but she could not. Not if she did not want to starve on the road.

She had to keep going.

Broke and alone. It didn't matter.

She was free.

Louisa smiled and continued to walk.

Chapter 4: William

A gentle breeze stirred the leaves of the ancient oak trees that covered the path leading to Lord Blackwood's quiet estate.

The rhythmic clopping of the carriage horses faded into the distance as Lord Blackwood stepped onto the familiar cobblestone road.

Relief washed over him, a sweet contrast to the suffocating atmosphere of London.

"Welcome back, Lord Blackwood. It's been so long!" boomed a man with a salt-and-pepper beard rivaling the bushes lining the path.

This was Edgar, the Earl's loyal butler, a man who had served his family for decades.

More than just an employee, Edgar was a confidante, a source of unwavering support, and family.

"Edgar," William replied, a genuine smile gracing his lips for the first time in a long while. "It's good to be back."

He handed his traveling cloak to Edgar, nostalgia tugging at his heart.

Gone were the dull uniforms and powdered wigs of the London elite.

Here, comfort and familiarity reigned supreme.

"Anything interesting happen while I was away?" William inquired as they walked towards the imposing manor house.

Edgar chuckled, a twinkle in his eye. "Aside from Mrs. Higgins' prized rose bush being ravaged by a rogue rabbit, nothing too out of the ordinary, my lord."

William laughed, the sound echoing through the quiet grounds.

"I'm sure Mrs. Heather has a warm pot of tea waiting for you along with your favorite biscuits."

Mrs. Heather, the estate's kind housekeeper, was another cornerstone of William's life here.

Her unfailing warmth and delicious cooking had been a haven during his late wife's illness.

After a refreshing cup of tea and a plate of Mrs. Heather's warm scones, an idea sparked in his mind.

"Edgar," he began, "I have a task for you."

Edgar straightened. "Whatever you require, Lord William."

"I wish to reopen the bookstore," William declared. "The one that was closed after ... after Anna's passing."

A flicker of sadness crossed Edgar's face, a shared grief for the kind woman who had graced the manor with her laughter, but it was quickly replaced by a spark of enthusiasm.

"A splendid idea, Lord William! The bookstore was always a source of great joy for you and Lady Anna. It would be a fitting tribute to her memory."

"Indeed," William agreed, a sad smile playing on his lips. "But we need the right person to run it. Mr. Abernathy, the previous proprietor ... is he still in the area?"

"Ah. Mr. Abernathy," Edgar mused, stroking his chin thoughtfully. "Let me check the local bar. I wouldn't be surprised if he's still around. He was quite attached to the bookstore as well."

True to Edgar's word, within a few hours, they managed to track down Mr. Abernathy. He was a sprightly old man with twinkling eyes and a mane of white hair atop his head. A wide grin spread across his face the moment he caught sight of William.

"Lord Blackwood! Fancy seeing you back here! And looking ... well, healthier than the last time we met," Mr. Abernathy said.

William chuckled. "Mr. Abernathy, I'm glad you remember me. I have a proposition for you."

They proceeded to the dusty confines of the bookstore, a space William knew well. The scent of old paper and leather filled the air—a familiar comfort. Cobwebs draped the corners, and a layer of dust coated the shelves that had once overflowed with books.

William sighed in sadness.

He should never have left. What was he thinking going back to London?

"Well, well." Mr. Abernathy whistled, his eyes twinkling. "Looks like we have our work cut out for us, wouldn't you say, my lord?"

William joined him in a smile. They spent the next hour walking through the store, taking stock of what needed to be done: a fresh coat of paint, some new furniture, and of course, restocking the shelves with a diverse selection of literature.

"We'll need a good mix of classics and new releases," Lord Blackwood noted, running his finger across a dusty shelf. "And perhaps a section dedicated to local history."

Mr. Abernathy's eyes sparkled. "Excellent idea, Lord William! There's a wealth of stories waiting to be unearthed in these parts."

As they continued their discussion, William felt a sense of peace settling over him. Here, surrounded by the familiar scent of books and the camaraderie with Mr. Abernathy, he felt truly alive. This wasn't the suffocating world of London society, where titles and fortune were the only currency. This was his haven, a place where he could rediscover his love for knowledge and connect with people who shared his passion.

He looked around the bookstore, picturing it filled with eager patrons browsing the shelves, their faces lit by the warm glow of strategically placed lamps. He imagined engaging in conversations about philosophy, history, and the latest literary sensation.

A warmth bloomed in his chest, a sense of purpose he hadn't felt since Anna's passing.

***

The evening sun cast long shadows across the dusty shelves of Blackwood Books as William and Mr. Abernathy continued their work.

The air hung heavy with the comforting scent of old paper, and sunlight filtering through the patched-up windows illuminated a whirlwind of swirling dust motes.

Every creak of the floorboards and groan of a weary bookshelf felt like a symphony of revival to William's ears.

Here, amidst forgotten tales and whispered histories, he finally felt a sense of belonging.

Their task was far from complete. Warped shelves craved sturdy replacements, broken display cases needed resurrection, and the faded floral wallpaper begged for a refresh.

Yet, William reveled in the prospect of restoring this literary haven. He envisioned tall, well-stocked shelves groaning under the weight of knowledge, comfortable reading nooks bathed in warm lamplight, and the sweet melody of turning pages filling the air.

As dusk began to settle, Mr. Abernathy, his eyes gleaming with youthful enthusiasm, announced, "Well, Lord Blackwood, for one day, that's enough progress for an old man. Tomorrow, we tackle the dusty corners and forgotten treasures!"

William chuckled, a genuine sound that echoed through the large space. "Mr. Abernathy, I have a feeling this will be an ongoing adventure, not just a task."

Bidding farewell to Mr. Abernathy for the evening, William stepped out of the bookstore and into the cool embrace of the twilight. He inhaled deeply, filling his lungs with the crisp air that carried the faint scent of woodsmoke and wildflowers. A peaceful sigh escaped his lips as he started his walk back to the manor.

Suddenly, a notice tacked to a weathered wooden post caught his eye. He stopped, his brows furrowing as he read the bold, black text: "Missing Heiress – Reward Offered."

Below the text, a crude drawing depicted a young woman in a flowing blue gown, the very same cerulean blue gown he'd seen at the ball. The mask too.

A jolt of shock ran through him. The emerald eyes, the fiery spirit, the disdain for Lord Thorne... it all clicked into place.

William guessed that was how she looked when she ran away, so it made sense.

The captivating woman he had danced with, the one who ran away, was none other than Lady Louisa Hastings, the missing heiress.

The drawing was a caricature at best, but the unmistakable detail of the sapphire necklace she wore during their dance confirmed his suspicion.

His mind raced. Was her disappearance a planned scheme to escape Lord Thorne, or was she genuinely in danger?

A pang of concern tugged at his heart. The woman who had intrigued him with her wit and defiance could be in dire straits.

He wasn't sure he could ignore it. He had to find out more.

Back at the manor, he found Edgar tending to the rose bushes that had been ravaged by the rogue rabbit. "Edgar," he called out, his voice urgent. "I need your help."

Edgar straightened, a twig clutched in his hand. "Is something wrong, my lord?"

William recounted his encounter with the missing heiress poster and his growing worry for her. "I fear something is amiss," he concluded.

Edgar's face grew serious. "Missing, you say? This does sound concerning. Perhaps we should inquire at the local constable's office tomorrow."

William nodded, pacing a path on the grassy lawn. "Indeed. But first, I have another idea."

He disappeared into the manor house and returned with a heavy, leather-bound book tucked under his arm.

It was a directory of London's nobility.

With Edgar at his side, he spent the rest of the evening meticulously searching for any mention of Lady Louisa Hastings.

Their search yielded a few tidbits. Lady Louisa, as the first daughter, was the only heir to the considerable Hastings fortune, a fact that made her prime target for men like Lord Thorne.

Her parents, it turned out, had tragically passed away when she was very young, leaving her and her younger sister under the care of a cruel and controlling relative.

The more he learned about Lady Louisa's situation, the more determined he became to help. But how? He couldn't simply waltz into London and announce his suspicions. He needed a plan, a way to discreetly investigate the situation without drawing attention to himself or jeopardizing Louisa's safety.

But at the end of the day, he couldn't do much.

He didn't want to ever go back to London.

Not for any reason.

He could only look for her around here.

He would keep an eye out for a Lady Louisa Hastings.

Chapter 5: Louisa

Thorns snagged at Louisa's gown, the once elegant cerulean silk now a tattered mess.

Every rustle of leaves sent a jolt of fear through her, and every snap of a twig amplified the pounding of her heart.

How long had she been running? Hours, surely. Hours filled with adrenaline-fueled bursts of speed followed by periods of bone-deep exhaustion.

She needed to drop ... soon, or her body would stop obeying her.

She cursed under her breath, the words muffled by the damp cloth clinging to her face.

"This ... this ... this blasted gown!" she snapped and then regretted using all her strength for that outburst. She tugged at the tangled mess that threatened to trip her. "Perfect for a ball, useless for escaping an unwanted marriage!"

Louisa pushed on, her legs screaming in protest. The dense undergrowth tore at her exposed skin, leaving angry red welts in its wake.

Yet, the thought of those carriages coming after her, their intentions unmistakable, propelled her onward.

Finally, the oppressive grip of the forest began to loosen. Sunlight filtered through the gaps between the trees, dappling the forest floor in a mosaic of light and shadow. With a burst of renewed energy, Louisa emerged from the tangled undergrowth.

And there it was. A small, weathered wooden signboard, its paint faded but its message legible: "Welcome to Havenwood."

Relief washed over her in a tidal wave, so much it brought tears to her eyes.

Havenwood, a quiet town known for its friendly folk and peaceful demeanor.

A very different life compared to the life she'd left behind in London—a life filled with grasping relatives and suffocating expectations.

Louisa sank to the ground, the rough bark biting into her back. A sob escaped her lips, a mixture of exhaustion, fear, and the overwhelming joy of finding safety.

She closed her eyes, the gentle murmur of a nearby stream a soothing melody to her frayed nerves.

Havenwood. Here, she could start again. Here, she could shed the gilded cage of Lady Louisa Hastings and simply become Louisa, a woman seeking a life beyond her title and fortune.

Life here would be easy.

She groaned. What was she thinking?

Life here would be easy?

Pfft.

The weight of relief that had settled on Louisa began to waver as the reality of her situation set in.

She was a runaway heiress, alone and penniless. The grand gown, once a symbol of her societal standing, now felt like a huge burden.

All the money she had brought with her? Gone.

But was she about to give up?

No.

Louisa straightened her back, defiance in her eyes. She wouldn't let fear paralyze her.

First things first: shelter.

She scanned the dusty main street of Havenwood, her gaze finally landing on wooden sign with worn painted lettering: "Haven Inn."

Goodness.

She took a deep breath and walked toward it.

Pushing open the creaky door, she was assaulted by the rank smell of stale tobacco smoke mixed with carbolic soap and turpentine.

A lone man sat hunched behind a dusty counter, his eyes narrowing at her entrance.

His gaze took in her tattered clothing and disheveled hair, a clear question hanging in the air.

Other patrons, mostly men in work clothes, paused mid-conversation to gawk at her.

A gruff voice boomed from behind a dusty reception desk, "Can I help you?"

Louisa straightened her back, mustering every ounce of her aristocratic demeanor, and walked toward the man. "Excuse me," she said, her voice hoarse from disuse. "Do you have a room available for the night?"

The man behind the counter, a burly fellow with a receding hairline, scrutinized her without a word. The silence stretched, thick with tension. Louisa felt her cheeks flush under the weight of their stares.

Finally, the man grunted. "One night? Eight shillings."

Eight shillings. It was a laughably small sum compared to the life she'd known, but a fortune in her current predicament. She had no purse, no money, nothing but the clothes on her back, and a single valuable remaining.

Tucking her hand into the hidden pocket stitched into her undergarment, Louisa retrieved a delicate silver necklace. It was a cherished memento, a gift from her late mother, but survival trumped sentimentality.

"I have this," she said, placing the necklace on the counter.

The man snatched it, leaving a smudge on the silver. "Don't know much about jewelry, lady," he drawled as he eyed it. "But it looks fancy enough. Pawn it tomorrow. You get a room for the night."

Louisa swallowed the lump in her throat. It was a gamble—a painful one—but she had no other options. "Alright," she agreed, her voice barely a whisper.

He set the necklace on the table and tossed a set of rusty keys at her. "Room 12. Don't expect much."

Relief washed over Louisa. A roof over her head, even in this less-than-ideal establishment, was a victory. Ignoring the man's snide remark, she clutched the necklace and key in her hand and made a silent promise to herself. This was a temporary setback. In Havenwood, she would find a way to reclaim her life, one step, one pawnbroker transaction, at a time.

Louisa unlocked the door to room 12 with a tremor in her hand. The key turned with a rusty groan, and again her senses were assaulted by a stale wave of air thick with the smell of old tobacco and something vaguely floral that had long since lost its freshness.

The room was obviously neglected. A single small lamp for light, and peeling wallpaper that sported a lot of questionable stains.

A threadbare bed sat in the corner, its lumpy mattress promising a night of restless sleep.

A rickety wooden chair stood next to a chipped porcelain sink, and in the far corner, a grimy window offered a sliver of a view.

Exhaustion, however, took over. She didn't care if the room looked like it belonged to a ghost.

Collapsing onto the creaky bed, Louisa kicked off her mud-caked shoes, the sound echoing in the cramped space.

Despite the dinginess, the room offered a precious sense of security. Here, she could lock the door, shut out the world, and steal a few precious hours of sleep.

Her eyelids felt heavy, threatening to clamp shut, when a sudden commotion outside jolted her awake.

Curiosity piqued, she dragged herself towards the window, ignoring the protesting groans of the floorboards.

With much effort, she wrestled the rusty latch open. A cool breeze carrying the faint scent of pine needles washed over her face, a welcome respite from the stale air of the room. Below, the narrow street bustled with a flurry of activity.

Then, Louisa saw it. A vivid poster plastered onto an old lamppost across the street screamed her name: "Have You Seen Lady Louisa Hastings? Missing Heiress – Reward Offered."

Her heart lurched in her chest, a cold dread crawling down her spine.

There she was, her face staring back at her from the crudely drawn sketch.

The blue gown, torn but familiar, and the defiant set of her jaw, were all captured in exaggerated strokes. Panic clawed at her throat.

Suddenly, the stares of the men at the inn, the gruffness of the receptionist ... it all made sense.

Perhaps the news had reached Havenwood faster than she'd anticipated.

Here, in this supposed haven, she wasn't safe. Her carefully constructed plan lay shattered, her escape route abruptly cut off.

Despair threatened to engulf her, but a flicker of stubbornness sparked in her emerald eyes.

No. She wouldn't let them win. She had to disappear again, deeper, further ... somewhere they wouldn't think to look.

But how? She needed to be smarter this time.

Staying in Havenwood was no longer an option. It seemed her journey for freedom had just taken a sharp turn into territory she never thought existed.

Sleep, a luxury she desperately craved, would have to wait.

She needed a new plan. A daring one.

With a thief's eye, Louisa scanned the cramped inn room.

Thankfully, the previous occupant, a burly construction worker by the looks of the discarded boots by the bed, had left behind a pair of worn but sturdy trousers and a faded work shirt.

Ah ... she had been about to complain about the state of the room before, but now, with the devious plan running through her head, she couldn't help but smile.

Relief washed over her. This was far from ideal, but it was infinitely better than attracting attention in her tattered gown.

The room offered a single battered washbasin, barely enough for a cleaning.

She removed her soiled gown, the once elegant blue silk now a testament to her escape, and scrubbed it with a sliver of soap retrieved from the stained sink before using it to wash the dirt from her body.

Tears welled in her eyes as she saw the remnants of her former life swirling down the drain, but she forced them back.

Survival demanded sacrifice, and sentimentality was a luxury she couldn't afford.

This had to be done if she wanted to survive.

***

Dawn arrived, casting a pale, watery light upon the room. Louisa, exhausted but determined, stood before the cracked mirror.

Her once long, beautiful, flowing hair was now a shorter, boyish style that framed her face in a way that felt both unfamiliar and surprisingly liberating, no matter how uneven the cuts.

The elegant blue gown was gone, replaced by the worn work shirt and trousers borrowed from the previous occupant of the room.

While the clothes hung loosely on her slender frame, they achieved the desired effect: she looked like a young man, albeit a slightly bedraggled one.

The once-elegant lady was gone, replaced by a young man with a determined glint in his eyes. "Louis," she murmured, christening her new persona.

A name borrowed from her actual name. Nothing too serious, and something she could get familiar with fast.

The little sum of coins, gotten from the greasy spoon cafe down the street in exchange for her washed gown, wouldn't last long.

Louisa, now Louis, needed to find a way to survive. And fast.

There was only one remaining item of value—the delicate silver necklace her mother had gifted her.

A pang of sorrow struck her heart at what she was about to do, but there was no going back.

She would come back for her jewelry. She swore it.

Heaving a sigh, she ventured out of the room, the rickety floorboards groaning under her unfamiliar gait.

The gruff inn owner, thankfully oblivious to her transformation, merely grunted a goodbye as she exited the building, not knowing she was the lady from the night before, her precious necklace in her pocket, and the borrowed clothes clinging to her slender frame.

Louisa needed to move quickly. She had to disappear before anyone recognized her.

Not that they would with her new appearance, but she was too scared to just let loose.

Taking a deep breath, Louisa steeled herself. This was a sacrifice she had to make.

With the necklace nestled in her palm, Louis ventured deeper into Havenwood and soon spotted a dingy storefront with three gilded balls hanging above the door—a pawnshop.

She felt a flicker of hope ignite.

Surely, this would be the answer to her immediate woes.

Pushing open the creaky door, a bell jangled above her head, announcing her arrival.

The air inside was stale and thick with the smell of dust and desperation.

Behind a cluttered counter sat a wizened old man, his eyes like two dull marbles peering over spectacles perched precariously on his nose.

Louisa approached the counter, her heart pounding a frantic rhythm against her ribs. "Excuse me, sir," she said, her voice a low murmur.

The old man grunted, his gaze flickering from Louisa to the necklace clutched in her hand. With a bony claw, he reached for it and examined it with a disdainful sniff. He turned it over in his hands, his touch cold and impersonal.

"Silver," he rasped, his voice dry as parchment. "Tarnished at that. Not worth much in this condition, I'm afraid."

Louisa's stomach lurched.

What! What was the old man saying!

Her precious gift wasn't worth much?

Her small hope plummeted faster than a stone dropped down a well. "But it's ..." she began, then stopped.

She couldn't explain its value. He wouldn't understand.

"Ten coins," the old man declared, his voice flat. "Take it or leave it."

Ten coins.

It was barely enough for a night at the wretched inn, let alone a decent meal.

Fury rose within Louisa, battling with the cold grip of desperation.

This wasn't just about the money; it was about the blatant disrespect for her cherished keepsake.

With a newfound resolve, Louisa straightened her borrowed clothes, her chin jutting out in defiance. "Thank you for your time, sir," she said, her voice surprisingly steady. "I believe I'll keep it."

The old man watched her go, his rheumy eyes narrowing in what might've been annoyance or surprise.

Louisa didn't care.

She slammed the door shut behind her, the sound echoing through the deserted street.

Disappointment threatened to engulf her, but she wouldn't give in.

There had to be another way.

Right?

How else would she survive?

As she walked, kicking at a stray pebble in frustration, a bookshop, nestled between a bakery and a cobbler's shop, caught her eye.

An idea sparked in her mind.

Pushing open the creaky door, a comforting wave of the scent of old paper and leather enveloped her, tugging at a forgotten memory.

A tall, portly man with kind eyes looked up from behind a cluttered counter.

"Welcome, young sir," he boomed, his voice surprisingly gentle. "Can I interest you in a rare first edition, perhaps?"

Louisa swallowed the lump in her throat. She hadn't planned on this detour, but desperation fueled her courage. "Actually, sir," she began, lowering her voice to a more masculine register, "I'm looking for work. Any work, really."

The man's eyebrows shot up in surprise. "Work? Here?" He chuckled, a pleasant sound that filled the cozy shop. "We don't get many people seeking employment. Not in a bookstore, that is."

Louisa straightened her shoulders, projecting a confidence she didn't entirely feel. "I'm a quick learner, sir. I can read, and write, and I'm strong enough to carry your heaviest tomes." She wasn't entirely lying. Her years of private tutoring had equipped her with at least those skills.

The man, Mr. Abernathy, as the nameplate on his chest proclaimed, studied her with a thoughtful gaze. "Hmm. A bit rough around the edges, aren't we?" he mused. "But you seem eager."

Louisa, sensing a potential lifeline, pressed her case further. "I'm willing to start at the bottom, sir. Sweeping floors, dusting shelves ... anything you need. Just give me a chance."

Mr. Abernathy seemed to ponder for a moment, then a smile crinkled the corners of his eyes. "Alright, young man," he said. "You've got yourself a job. Start by unpacking those new arrivals over there. And you call me Mr. Abernathy."

Relief flooded Louisa's veins.

A job.

A roof over her head, even if temporary. It wasn't ideal, but it was a start.

Louisa threw herself into her new role with a fervor that surprised even herself.

Shelves were meticulously dusted, books carefully sorted, and orders filled with an efficiency that left Mr. Abernathy blinking in surprise.

Louisa, fueled by both necessity and a newfound passion for the world of words, devoured any spare moments she had, nose buried in a dusty tome.

Her quick grasp of literature and her ability to recall obscure facts impressed Mr. Abernathy more with each passing day.

One afternoon, Louisa found herself staring at the dusty display window.

There were few customers, and she couldn't just work here with no one coming into the bookshop.

She needed to do something.

A wave of inspiration struck her.

With borrowed chalk and a flourish of artistic license, she sketched a lovely scene on the windowpane—a knight slaying a monstrous dragon guarding a mountain of books.

Beneath it, she scrawled in bold lettering: "Havenwood Bookshop – Where Adventures Await!"

Mr. Abernathy, initially skeptical, chuckled at her handiwork.

However, his amusement turned to astonishment when a steady stream of curious townsfolk began pouring into the shop, drawn by the window display.

Louisa tried as much as possible to be calm, but she couldn't, not when everyone seemed to gossip about the missing heiress and that they'd love to find her.

She was fidgety all day long.

Sales soared, and a previously unknown sense of purpose bloomed within her.

That evening, as the last rays of the setting sun cast long shadows across the bookstore floor, Louisa perched on a stool behind the counter, carefully dusting a row of leather-bound classics.

Mr. Abernathy, nestled in his usual armchair by the window, was engrossed in a well-worn copy of Don Quixote.

The shop had finally emptied, leaving a comfortable quiet that settled over them like a familiar blanket.

A sigh escaped Louisa's lips.

While the past few hours had flown by in a whirlwind of activity, a nagging worry gnawed at the back of her mind.

The small coin she had earned from selling her gown was dwindling fast, barely enough for another night at the dingy inn.

The thought of returning to that cramped, stifling room filled her with dread.

Stealing a glance at Mr. Abernathy, Louisa saw him turn a page with a contented sigh.

Taking a deep breath, she decided to broach the subject. "Mr. Abernathy," she began, her voice tentative, "this place ... it's been wonderful. I can't thank you enough for the opportunity."

Mr. Abernathy looked up, a smile crinkling the corners of his eyes. "Nonsense, Louis. You've been a tremendous help. The shop feels ... alive again, thanks to your efforts."

Louisa felt a warmth bloom in her chest. "It's the least I could do," she mumbled. "But ... well, the truth is, I was wondering ..."

Mr. Abernathy placed his book down on the armrest, his gaze gentle. "Wondering about what, my son?"

Louisa hesitated for a moment, then blurted out, "I have to pay for another night at the inn, and ... well, my funds are running a bit low."

A look of understanding dawned on Mr. Abernathy's face.

He leaned forward, his voice dropping to a low murmur. "That dreadful place, isn't it? No fit accommodation for someone like you, especially not someone who brightens my bookshop like a ray of sunshine."

Louisa shifted uncomfortably under his kind gaze. "It's just temporary, sir. Until I get back on my feet."

Mr. Abernathy chuckled. "On your feet, eh? You've already landed there, Louis. More firmly than you might realize. Here's the thing," he continued, leaning closer, "I've been thinking. You have a keen mind for literature, a sharp wit, and an undeniable talent for sales. I wouldn't mind having an apprentice under my wing ... someone to help me run this haven of stories."

Louisa's jaw dropped. "An apprentice? But ... me?"

"Why not?" Mr. Abernathy countered, a twinkle in his eye. "You'd have a proper room here, comfortable and safe. Meals included, of course. And a small stipend to tide you over. What do you say?"

Relief washed over Louisa in a tidal wave.

This was a chance to stay, to learn, to build a new life. "Mr. Abernathy, that would be a dream come true," she said, her voice thick with emotion.

A wide smile spread across Mr. Abernathy's face. "Excellent! Then it's settled. Welcome aboard, Miss ... I mean, Mr. Apprentice."

Louisa couldn't help but grin, a genuine, heartfelt smile that reached her eyes.

The bookstore, once a refuge, had become something more—a home. But the quiet celebration was short-lived.

A sudden chill swept through the shop as the bell above the door chimed, shattering the peaceful evening. Louisa turned, her smile fading as a tall, imposing figure stepped through the doorway.

His face, obscured by the shadow of a wide-brimmed hat, seemed perpetually shrouded.

The hat itself, a dark-felt monstrosity adorned with a single raven feather, seemed to radiate an aura of menace. He stepped inside, the shop's warm light finally revealing a pair of dark eyes with unsettling rims of grey.

Instinct, honed by weeks of fear and flight, screamed a warning within Louisa.

Her breath caught in her throat, and a cold hand of dread gripped her heart.

Goodness. Was this how her life would be?

Always scared?

She hoped not.

Chapter 6: William

The first, soft light of dawn painted the sky a pale rose as a gentle rapping sounded at William's chamber door.

Unlike the frantic callings of bustling London mornings, this was a soft knock, a signal of the quiet routine that now governed his life.

One more time, he wondered why he ever thought he could fit into the crazy London life.

He stretched languidly, the crisp linen sheets cool against his bare skin.

The sunlight streamed freely through simple muslin curtains, bathing the room in a soft glow.

A low voice called out, "My lord, it is Thomas."

Oh, the young butler who had begged to follow him from London.

William responded with a hearty, "Come in, Thomas."

The door opened slightly, and a young man with a mop of unruly brown hair and an endearingly nervous smile entered the chamber.

He was going to be William's new valet, and the young lad seemed to be taking his job quite seriously, no matter how inexperienced.

Thomas, however, made up for his inexperience with a genuine warmth and a willingness to please.

Thomas walked in, carrying a silver tray with a steaming pot of tea, a plate of sliced peaches, and a bowl of creamy porridge. "Good morning, my lord," he beamed, placing the tray on a small table beside the bed.

"Good morning, Thomas," William replied, sitting up. "Did you sleep well?"

"Like a log, my Lord," Thomas said. "The air here is so fresh, it puts you right to sleep. I knew I made the right decision to follow you."

William chuckled. "Indeed, it does. Now, help me with my dressing gown, would you?"

Thomas scurried forward with said gown and draped it over the lord's shoulders. Then he stopped, his hands hovering near William as if unsure where to touch.

William, with a touch of amusement, guided him through the simple process of putting his robe on him.

He washed his face and headed back to his bed where his breakfast waited.

Breakfast was a quiet affair, punctuated only by the clinking of china and the soft chirping of birds outside.

As William savored his tea, a sense of peace settled over him. No pressing engagements, no social calls—just the simple pleasure of starting the day with a nourishing meal.

After breakfast, Thomas led Lord Blackwood to his study, a cozy room lined with worn leather chairs and a large oak desk. Here, Edgar awaited him, holding a leather-bound journal and several neatly arranged parchments.

"Good morning, Lord Blackwood," Edgar greeted, a hint of a smile crinkling the corners of his eyes. "Did the young lad serve you well?"

"A beautiful morning it is, Edgar," William replied and then glanced at Thomas who looked nervous. "He did. I am pleased with his service."

He sat by his chair and dismissed the young lad so he could break his fast. "What news do you bring?"

Edgar cleared his throat. "The solicitor has finalized the transfer of the estate's surplus funds, my Lord. As discussed, a portion has been allocated to the restoration of the bookstore."

William nodded, excitement dancing in his eyes. His bookstore was slowly becoming an obsession.

"This, my lord," Edgar continued, unfolding a parchment, "is the information you requested regarding the establishment of your cocoa import company."

William took the document, his brow furrowing in concentration as he scanned the facts and figures. The idea of venturing into the cocoa trade had been brewing in his mind for some time. It was a strategic move, a way to diversify his income and inject some intellectual stimulation into his life.

He reviewed market trends, potential suppliers, and projected profit margins. Despite the potential benefits, a nagging doubt persisted. He wasn't a man of commerce, nor was he a scholar with an insatiable thirst for knowledge. Books, however, were a different story. Books gave him an escape from reality.

An escape he really needed now.

He looked up from the parchment, his gaze drifting toward the window, where a gentle breeze stirred the leaves of the old oak trees outside.

"Edgar," he said, setting the cocoa report aside, "I believe I have a different task for you today."

Edgar's eyebrows rose in surprise. "Indeed, my lord?"

"Prepare the carriage," William declared with enthusiasm in his voice. "We're going to the bookstore."

Edgar, despite his initial surprise, nodded in agreement. William's love for the bookshop was no secret, and Edgar understood the peace it brought him. Besides, there were repairs to oversee and decisions to be made—perfect tasks for a lord seeking solace in the familiar embrace of books.

As the carriage clattered down the gravel driveway, William closed his eyes for a moment. He might not be the bookish scholar he yearned to be, but in the dusty shelves and comforting silence of Blackwood Books, he found a different kind of solace, a sense of belonging he hadn't known he craved. It was a sanctuary in more ways than one, a place where he could shed the weight of his title and simply be William, a man seeking refuge in the written word.

***

Later, the carriage bounced along the familiar path, the rhythmic clopping of the horses a comforting soundtrack to the Earl's thoughts.

As they rounded a corner, a splash of red caught his eye. There it was, plastered on a weathered noticeboard as it had been for several days: a "Missing Heiress" poster featuring Lady Louisa Hastings.

Disappointment washed over him. Days had passed, and Lady Louisa Hastings remained missing.

Why did it have to be her?

He couldn't shake the image of her fiery green eyes and the defiance etched on her face as they danced.

He sighed, pushing the troubling thoughts aside. He would discreetly inquire about the missing woman later.

As they pulled up in front of the building, a sense of anticipation buzzed through Lord Blackwood. The prospect of working alongside Mr. Abernathy, poring over dusty tomes and discussing forgotten classics, filled him with a peculiar joy.

He leaped out of the carriage, a wide smile stretching across his face.

However, what he saw made him stop short, a frown marring his forehead.

Right in front of the bookstore, a very fragile, thin-looking young man—maybe a teenager—emerged from the store, and the scene that unfolded made William blink in startled surprise.

The young man, humming an off-key tune and seemingly lost in a world of his own, was attempting to haul a precariously tall stack of books toward the storefront.

Lord Blackwood opened his mouth to let him know that the books were probably twice the lad's size and could easily make him fall, but it was too late. His warning hung in the air as the precarious stack tilted.

With a yelp so high pitched it could have rivaled a startled cat, the young man lunged forward, arms flailing wildly. But it was too late. Books cascaded down like a papery rain, engulfing the young man in a cloud of dust and forgotten stories.

"Easy there, lad!" Lord Blackwood, unable to stifle a chuckle, rushed forward trying to help, but before he could reach him, the young man held up equally fragile and dainty fingers, eyes wide with what looked like fear.

"Stop!"

The earl screeched to a halt in confusion. "I'm trying to help you."

"N-no need," the lad said in a soft voice, and William decided he had to be in pain. The lad, however, held up his hand higher as if not trusting Lord Blackwood to stay put. "T-thank you, but I can help myself."

William tilted his head to the side. The lad wore clothes that were worn and obviously from the slums, but he still managed to speak so well.

Why was he so skittish? Did he have something to hide?

William narrowed his eyes at the lad but didn't say anything.

After a low groan of discomfort, the lad was finally able to stand.

When he looked up, William froze.

He wasn't even sure why. But there was something ... something about the lad that tugged at his heart, and it confused him.

Sharp green eyes, a lean face, soft plump lips, no facial hair whatsoever, so obviously a teenager. Not many men looked like this.

He knew Madam Frank would kill to have a lad like this walk down the street wearing her designs.

The boy looked so lean but healthy at the same time.

Curious, he watched the young man disentangle himself from the literary debris, brushing stray pages out of his mop of unruly auburn hair before hastily pushing his cap back on.

Then he looked up. His green eyes widened in surprise and again what looked like fear.

He had to be hiding something.

"Oh! Uh! Good morning, sir!" the young man exclaimed, nearly toppling the fallen stacks of books in his haste to attend to Lord Blackwood.

Lord Blackwood's hands shot forward but stayed when he remembered the lad didn't want to be touched.

The young boy scrambled to pick up the books. "W-welcome to Blackwood Books! Can I interest you in ... uh ..." He looked up at William again and flushed. "Anything?"

William's surprise deepened. The boy's voice, a touch higher pitched but with a familiar lilt, sent a strange jolt through him.

"I'd like to enter the store first?" he said, amused, and the lad flushed again.

"Oh! Right! This way, sir!" He pointed at the door and gave a small bow.

William chuckled and pushed open the creaky bookstore door and was met with a sight that startled him.

Gone were the dusty cobwebs and stagnant air of the days before. Sunlight streamed through newly patched windows, illuminating a surprising transformation.

Bookshelves, though still bearing signs of wear, were neatly arranged, their once-chaotic contents meticulously organized.

A fresh coat of paint on the walls replaced the faded floral wallpaper, and a large rug, woven with a vibrant floral pattern, warmed the previously bare wooden floor.

It seemed the lad had been quite busy.

When his eyes landed on the boy, William found him already staring.

"You look ready to bolt," he commented and watched as a look of utter bewilderment crossed the lad's face, followed by a hilariously awkward attempt to regain his composure.

"I ... I apologize, sir," he stammered, brushing a stray lock of hair from his small, shiny forehead. "The surprise of seeing a customer ... well, I haven't quite mastered the art of bookstore greetings yet. Or anything at all. I'm new."

Ah, that had to be it.

William chuckled. "No need to apologize," he said, his amusement growing. "I should have announced myself. I'm looking to browse some books."

"I'm Louis," the young man said, dusting off his trousers. "Mr. Abernathy's new assistant."

"Louis. A pleasure," William replied, his smile lingering a touch longer than necessary. "And where is Mr. Abernathy himself?"

"Oh." Louis's smile faltered. "Mr. Abernathy had to step out unexpectedly. Said something about a ... toothache, I believe."

William raised an eyebrow, a knowing smile playing on his lips. Mr. Abernathy, with his iron constitution, and a sudden toothache? It seemed more likely that the old bookseller had simply found a more urgent task to attend to.

But just as this thought occurred to him, it was interrupted by the creak of the old shop door.

Mr. Abernathy, his face flushed and hair askew, bustled in, a worried frown creasing his brow.

"My Lord William! What a surprise!" he exclaimed, his voice laced with excitement. "You haven't been here for two days, and I was starting to get worried."

Louis, who had seemed to be engrossed in his fingers in a forgotten corner, jumped a mile high immediately after the door opened, a small yell leaving his lips.

William turned and frowned.

Why was the boy so out of his skin?

"Oh! It's you, Mr. Abernathy!" he squeaked, cheeks burning a shade that rivaled the setting sun. "I thought ..."

William immediately latched on to that. "You thought what?"

Green eyes snapped up to his and widened before looking away. "N-nothing."

Something was very wrong, and William knew he would do anything to find out what it was.

Mr. Abernathy chuckled, walking over to ruffle the young man's already unruly hair, over his cap.

The boy did not pull away even though he flinched a little.

What was his problem?

Mr. Abernathy turned back to Lord Blackwood, mopping his brow with a handkerchief. "My apologies for being out. A toothache, most dreadful ... though perhaps a tad exaggerated," he admitted with a sheepish grin.

Lord Blackwood couldn't help but return the grin. "No worries, Mr. Abernathy," he leaned closer to the man. "Now, Mr. Abernathy," he began, his voice carefully neutral, "while I commend your kind heart, are you certain it's ... wise to employ a young man you found on the streets?"

"Ah, yes. Louis," Mr. Abernathy boomed, his voice taking on a grandfatherly tone. "A bright young lad, isn't he?"

He cleared his throat and prayed the old man wouldn't make things hard for him. "Maybe. But he's too fearful and jumpy ... I don't think he should be here."

Mr. Abernathy's brow furrowed in confusion. "Why, Louis is a gem! Sharp as a tack, and he has a genuine love for the written word. He's a natural fit around here, wouldn't you agree?"

"No." William tried to lower his voice even more, but he knew Louis could hear them anyway. "No, I wouldn't."

The air in the room grew thick with tension. Louis's hand clenched into a white-knuckled fist, but he said nothing.

"Look at him, Mr. Abernathy. Young, dressed in rags, but speaks so fluently, and looks so dainty. He looks like the rebellious type who runs from home."

"Excuse me?" Louis finally spoke up, scoffing.

Lord Blackwood sighed and turned to Louis. "You keep jumping at everything. If that's not suspicious, I don't know what is, and it screams bad luck."

Louis's eyes widened with a glare. "Bad luck, you say? It's men like you who make people like me live in fear. I'm just trying to make a living here!"

Silence.

Louis's outburst hung in the air, the anger barely contained. The earl, however, didn't seem fazed. A slow smile spread across his face.

Thank goodness the boy could hold his own. He would have sent him away otherwise.

"Whoa there," Lord Blackwood said, holding up his hands in mock surrender. "Didn't mean to strike a nerve. Actually," he continued, his eyes twinkling, "I think I find your passion rather refreshing."

Louis blinked, his anger sputtering out like a candle in a breeze. "R-Refreshing?" he stammered, unsure how to react.

"Absolutely," Lord Blackwood confirmed. "You see, most folks who jump at shadows wouldn't have the mind to stand up for themselves in situations like these. They would cower, and that almost always means they have things to hide."

"Well, I wouldn't say I stood up for myself..."

"You held your own," Lord Blackwood corrected. "And that, my friend," he added, his voice growing serious, "is precisely what I need in my shop. Someone with a bit of... fire."

Louis's jaw dropped. "W-wait," he stammered, "This... this store is yours?"

"Indeed, it is." His smile widened. "Welcome to my esteemed bookstore. Your new home away from home, shall we say?"

"T-that means you're keeping me?" Louis finally managed to ask, gesturing around at the shelves overflowing with books.

Lord Blackwood raised an eyebrow. "Was that ever in question? A little jumpy, perhaps, but you know your books and you have a way with words. Besides," he added, a playful glint in his eye, "you seem to attract a certain amount of excitement. The shop could use a bit of that."

He watched as the lad grinned. The fear that had been a constant companion for so long seemed to melt away, replaced by a flicker of hope. Maybe, just maybe, this wasn't such a bad idea after all.

Chapter 7: Louisa

Louisa dusted a first edition copy of "Tom Jones" with exaggerated care, a sly smile playing on her lips.

Ever since the gruff yet strangely intriguing William had revealed his true identity as the owner of Havenwood Bookshop, a delightful game of cat and mouse had commenced.

Their daily interactions had become a dance of witty banter and intellectual sparring, each barb carefully veiled but undeniably thrilling.

Today, William ambled in at his usual pre-closing time, his dark eyes scanning the shelves before settling on her.

"Busy day, apprentice?" he rumbled, his voice rough.

"Busy enough, Mr. Owner," she countered, winking. "Though nothing a good dose of Fielding can't cure."

William raised an eyebrow, a hint of amusement dancing in his eyes. "Fielding, eh? A bit bawdy for such a sunny afternoon, wouldn't you say?"

Louisa couldn't help but admire the way the late afternoon light glinted off the silver streaks in his dark hair.

Ignore the handsome owner, Louisa. Focus on the first edition, she mentally scolded herself.

"Bawdy, perhaps," she conceded, "but the social commentary is undeniably sharp. A bit like a well-aimed rapier, wouldn't you agree?"

"Sharp, indeed," he agreed, his voice dropping a notch lower.

He took a deliberate step closer, his presence filling the space between them. Louisa held his gaze, her heart hammering a frantic tattoo against her ribs.

Was he flirting? The very notion sent a shiver down her spine.

Oh Louisa, you are long gone, aren't you? She mused to herself. *You are Louis right now. There's no way the man's flirting with you.*

Thankfully, Mr. Abernathy, bless his oblivious soul, chose that moment to intervene. "Ah, William! Just the man I was looking for. I need your keen eye on this manuscript ..."

The tension evaporated as quickly as it had arisen.

Lord Blackwood sighed dramatically. "Another one, Abernathy? Must you tempt me with these dusty relics right before closing time?"

Louisa stifled a laugh as William followed Mr. Abernathy towards the back room, their bickering as familiar and comforting as an old book.

The playful hostility between them was undeniably entertaining, but a small, secret part of her longed for something more.

A week later, a different William entered the shop.

Gone was the gruff exterior—well, not entirely, but noticeable enough—replaced by a particular energy that made him seem strangely vulnerable. He cleared his throat, his gaze flitting around the room before landing on her.

"Louis," he began, his voice surprisingly hesitant, "well, I was wondering if you might be interested in accompanying me to the Historical Society's lecture on the recent decipherment of hieroglyphics this weekend?"

Louisa's heart skipped a beat. Was this ...?

"Hieroglyphics?" she teased, feigning disinterest. "Sounds positively scholarly, Mr. Owner."

The earl's cheeks gave way to a smile, a sight that made Louisa bite her lip to suppress hers.

"It's not just any lecture," he mumbled, avoiding her gaze. "They're discussing the groundbreaking work of Jean-François Champollion. Supposedly, he's cracked the code of those ancient Egyptian symbols."

Now, Louisa's interest was genuinely piqued. Champollion's work was a game-changer in the field of Egyptology, unlocking a treasure trove of knowledge about a lost civilization. "Champollion, you say. Now, that is intriguing."

A relieved smile spread across Lord Blackwood's face. "Excellent! So, you'll come?"

"Perhaps," she said, drawing out the word for dramatic effect. "But only if you promise to behave yourself and refrain from any ... rash acquisitions."

William, as much as she enjoyed his company, tended to get carried away during auctions.

He chuckled, the sound warm and genuine. "I can't guarantee anything around those fascinating artifacts, but I'll do my best."

The following Saturday found them seated in the stuffy auditorium of the Historical Society.

William, surprisingly, seemed captivated by the lecture, his brow furrowed in concentration as he scribbled notes. Louisa, however, found herself more captivated by the man beside her.

The way his sharp jawline tightened with focus, the way his dark hair fell across his forehead, the way his hand brushed against hers accidentally as they reached for the same program—all these seemingly trivial details sent a thrill coursing through her.

He was undeniably handsome, and the more she interacted with him, the more his gruff exterior seemed to melt away, revealing a surprisingly witty and intelligent man beneath.

As they exited the auditorium, William moved in step with her, walking right beside her, a move so natural it felt preordained. Louisa's breath hitched, and she stole a glance at him.

He looked normal, just staring straight ahead like he had no worries in the world.

Louisa's cheeks flushed, her gaze holding a nervous intensity that mirrored her feelings.

"So," he began, his voice husky, "what did you think of the lecture?"

Louisa, for once, let down her guard. The world seemed to shrink to just the two of them, the din of the dispersing crowd fading into background noise.

"Intriguing," she admitted, her voice low and vibrant. "Champollion's work is truly groundbreaking. Imagine, unlocking the secrets of an entire civilization through symbols carved into stone millennia ago."

William's surprise was evident. "You ... you actually followed the lecture?"

"Of course I did," she countered, a playful glint in her eyes. "Besides the obvious historical significance, think of the possibilities for deciphering ancient texts that might hold valuable knowledge—lost medicines, forgotten technologies ... who knows what secrets are waiting to be unearthed?"

William looked at her with something akin to awe. "You see things most people wouldn't. A connection between dusty hieroglyphs and ... business opportunities?"

Louisa couldn't help but grin. "Precisely. Imagine, William, if we could acquire a genuine artifact with an inscription—something decipherable, of course. Think of the publicity, the interest it would generate amongst collectors and scholars alike!"

A slow smile spread across Lord Blackwood's face. "You know, Mr. Apprentice," he drawled, his voice surprisingly warm, "you're far more than just a quick learner. You're a walking vault of fascinating ideas."

Louisa felt a blush creep up her neck. "Just doing my part to ensure the continued success of Havenwood Bookshop," she deflected, though a secret thrill ran through her. He was impressed.

Lord Blackwood hailed a waiting carriage, and as they settled inside, a comfortable silence fell between them. This time, it wasn't filled with tension, but with a sense of newfound connection. William, emboldened, began to speak of his childhood, of his fascination with ancient Egypt that had stemmed from a dusty book he'd discovered in his grandfather's library.

Louisa listened intently, enthralled by the glimpse into his life.

He spoke with a passion that surprised her, a vulnerability she hadn't expected from the gruff owner. For the first time, she felt a genuine connection with him, a desire to share her past. But the familiar knot of fear tightened in her stomach. No, she couldn't. Not yet. Not until she knew for sure she could trust him.

The carriage finally drew to a halt in front of the bookstore. As Louisa stepped out, she turned to face him, a wave of gratitude washing over her.

"Thank you, Lord Blackwood," she said. "For the lecture, for the ... conversation."

"The pleasure was entirely mine, Louis," he replied, his voice sincere.

Hope battled with fear within her.

She yearned to spend more time with this intriguing man.

But the memory of Lord Thorne, of his betrayal and the constant danger she knew was coming, kept her tongue-tied.

Just as she was about to say goodbye, a voice from the shadows startled them.

"Well, well, well, Lord Blackwood. Fancy meeting you here with ..." The man's voice trailed off as he focused on Louisa. "A ... new ... friend?"

Louisa's blood ran cold.

The man standing before them, his lips curled in a sneer, was a familiar face, one she would never forget. It was Mr. Hemmings, the magistrate who had been assigned to her missing case in London.

She had seen it in the daily papers.

What was he doing here?

Had they finally traced her here?

William, oblivious to Louisa's terror, straightened his shoulders and turned to the newcomer. "Hemmings. What a surprise. And this, my good fellow, is Mr. Apprentice, a valued employee of Havenwood Bookshop."

Mr. Hemmings' eyes narrowed, his gaze lingering on Louisa for a beat too long. "Interesting. Perhaps another time, then, William. Earl."

Louisa's face was drained of color. "Earl," she mumbled to herself, her voice barely a whisper.

The weight of the title slammed into her.

Panic surged through her, drowning out the rest of their conversation.

The gruff, book-loving William, the man who made her laugh and sparked a flicker of hope within her, was an earl. He was an aristocrat, a member of the very class that had ostracized and hunted her down.

Fear, cold and sharp, clawed at her throat. Lord Thorne's betrayal echoed in her mind, a dark stain on her past. Could William be the same? Was their newfound connection a mere game, a way to gain her trust before delivering her back to the clutches of the law?

She practically ran for the safety of her lodgings. Once inside, she collapsed onto the rickety bed, her heart hammering against her ribs.

Sleep eluded her that night. Every rustle outside sounded like approaching footsteps, every creak of the floorboards like pursuing voices. Had she been a fool for letting down her guard? For allowing herself to be charmed by the Earl of Blackwood?

The next day, a heavy cloud settled over her. The bookstore, once a refuge, now felt like a trap. The thought of facing William, of having to feign normalcy, filled her with dread. She scanned the schedule Mr. Abernathy kept behind the counter, her stomach churning as she saw William's usual pre-closing time marked with a familiar star.

There was no way she could face him. Not today. Taking a deep breath, she formulated a plan. Work. She'd bury herself in work, meticulously cataloguing the new shipment of books. Anything to avoid an encounter.

As the day wore on, her anxiety gnawed at her. Every creak of the door sent her heart into overdrive.

Mr. Abernathy, bless his obliviousness, didn't seem to notice her heightened state. He pottered about the shop, humming a cheerful tune as he dusted the shelves.

Just before closing time, the telltale chime of the bell shattered the relative peace. Louisa froze, her breath catching in her throat. She peeked around the corner of a towering bookcase, her heart sinking as she saw William's broad frame standing by the counter, a frown creasing his brow.

"Mr. Apprentice?" Mr. Abernathy's voice called out. "Where are you? Lord Blackwood is here."

Louisa winced at the title. Lord Blackwood. The very sound of it sent a feeling of fear through her.

"Coming, Mr. Abernathy!" She forced a cheerful tone into her voice, even though it sounded strained to her ears.

She took a deep breath, squaring her shoulders, and stayed completely rooted to the spot.

There was no way she was going out to meet William.

She waited and listened, but nothing.

Utter silence.

The silence stretched, thick with tension. William cleared his throat, then turned back to Mr. Abernathy.

They engaged in a brief conversation about a first edition they were trying to acquire, their voices a distant hum as Louisa focused on cataloging, her mind a churning vortex of fear and confusion.

When William finally left, a heavy silence descended upon the shop as Louisa finally stepped out to the front desk.

Mr. Abernathy, peering at her over his spectacles, tilted his head in concern.

"Mr. Apprentice," he began gently, "you seem ... troubled today. Is everything alright?"

Louisa forced a smile, the effort feeling akin to climbing a mountain. "Just a bit tired, Mr. Abernathy. A long day of organizing."

The lie stuck in her throat, but she couldn't bring herself to confide in him.

Not yet.

She didn't understand William, his motives, or the implications of his title.

Chapter 8: William

The scent of aged paper and worn leather, usually a balm to his soul, did little to quell the disquiet gnawing at Lord Blackwood's gut.

He stood outside the bookstore, watching through the window.

Inside, Louis, the young man he'd taken a chance on, had brought a spark of life back into the dusty shelves.

But the bookstore had nothing to do with why he was there that day. Tucked beneath his arm, nestled amongst rejection letters and forgotten dreams, lay a proposal.

A meticulously crafted proposal outlining his vision for a new cocoa venture. The problem? Securing the backing of a notoriously difficult French businessman, Monsieur Rousseau. A businessman with whom a well-spoken, and preferably French-speaking, companion would be invaluable.

He needed a brilliant mind with him.

His gaze drifted through the window, searching for the familiar mop of auburn hair again. There he was, Louis, perched on a ladder, meticulously dusting a shelf of antique novels. The very definition of unexpected, yet undeniably the perfect solution to William's predicament.

With a deep breath, he pushed open the door, the chime announcing his arrival. Louis turned, a smile lighting up his face as he saw William. That smile, however, faltered slightly as he noticed the tension apparent in William's face.

"Lord Blackwood? Everything alright?" Louis hopped down from the ladder, his small, beautiful face frowning with genuine concern.

William hesitated, the weight of the proposal and the upcoming meeting settling heavily on his shoulders.

"Louis," he began, his voice betraying a hint of apprehension, "I have a proposition for you."

He watched as curiosity flickered in Louis's eyes, a flicker quickly replaced by something else entirely—fear?

"It concerns ... business," William continued, choosing his words carefully. "There's a meeting I need to attend, a rather important one. And ..." He trailed off, taking another deep breath. "I could use someone to come with me."

Silence stretched between them, thick and heavy. Louis's initial apprehension had morphed into something far more complex. Hesitation, perhaps, a wariness battling with a nascent sense of determination. He opened his mouth to speak, but before any words could escape his lips, William continued, the decision suddenly clear in his mind.

"Look," William said, his voice softening, "this isn't some shady back-alley deal. It's ... it's a chance for me, a chance to build something new. And if you're willing, I could use your ... your intellect, your way with words, especially since the meeting will be ..." He hesitated, the name catching in his throat. "With a French businessman. Is this something you can do?"

***

An hour later, the carriage clattered to a halt outside the imposing granite building that housed Monsieur Rousseau's office.

William hopped down first, and then in a move etched into his brain, he turned and offered his hand to Louis, who also very calmly reached out, as if used to people helping him out of carriages, his fingers brushing William's palm.

A jolt of electricity shot up William's arm, a sensation far removed from the simple act of helping someone out of a carriage.

He frowned. Why did it feel so natural for Louis to take his hand?

And although he knew how fragile he was, touching his hand and seeing how soft it was?

He didn't know what to think.

Louis, however, seemed oblivious, his focus on disembarking with grace. He swung his leg out, aiming for the cobblestone street, but misjudged the height.

With a yelp, he began to topple forward. William's reflexes kicked in before his conscious mind could react. He shot out a hand, grabbing Louis firmly around the waist and pulling the lad flush against his chest.

They both froze.

Time seemed to slow. Louis, caught mid-fall, was suspended inches from the ground. Their bodies collided, the thin fabric of Louis's worn shirt doing little to shield William from the surprising curves hidden beneath.

A gasp escaped Louis's lips, his eyes widening in shock.

What? Curves?

He could feel the rapid thrum of Louis's pulse against his palm, the warmth radiating from his skin. Louis's hair, usually so unkempt, brushed against William's cheek, sending a shiver down his spine.

For a heartbeat—or maybe an eternity—they were frozen, locked in this unexpected embrace.

William found his gaze lingering on the soft curve of Louis's exposed neck.

Then, as quickly as it began, the moment shattered. Louis, his face flushed with a mixture of mortification and something else William couldn't decipher, scrambled away.

"D-don't touch me," he stammered, his voice breathless even as he glared at William.

Was it his imagination or did Louis have the curves of a female?

He cleared his throat, scoffing. "If I didn't touch you, lad, you'd be nursing a broken nose."

Why was he always so adamant about no touching? It wasn't normal.

"In that case, receive my thanks."

"No problem at all, Louis," he said, his voice slightly rougher than usual. "Let's just hope Monsieur Rousseau is as easy to catch as you were."

Louis shot him a wary glance, the blush still creeping up his neck. William couldn't help but return the look, his gaze lingering a beat too long on Louis's flushed face before forcing himself to look away.

As they walked into the office, the memory of Louis' tumble distracted him from his purpose. The unexpected brush of their bodies, the warmth, the lingering scent—it had ignited a fire within him that refused to be doused.

Yet, the flames danced around a confusing truth—Louis was an enigma.

What was happening? Was he running mad?

Short hair, worn clothes, a streetwise demeanor—everything about him screamed boy. But then there was the way he moved, a certain grace that hinted at something different.

The way his clothes hung on his slender frame, the way his voice dipped and rose with an eloquence that belied his supposed background.

The incident with the carriage had ripped away the veil for a fleeting moment, revealing a hint of feminine curves William couldn't shake.

Or maybe William was mistaken. That had to be it.

He realized that for the past few days, their arguments, once a source of annoyance, now took on a different flavor. William found himself seeking them out, relishing the spark in Louis's eyes, the way his voice rose in passionate defense.

He thrived on the intellectual sparring, the way Louis challenged him with his quick wit and sharp mind. It was infuriating and exhilarating all at once.

The worst part? He craved Louis's presence. The bookstore, once a refuge, now felt empty when Louis wasn't there, nose buried in a dusty tome or debating the merits of a particular author. He found himself making excuses to be near him, stealing glances that lingered a beat too long.

Guilt gnawed at him. What was he doing? Louis was an employee, a mystery, and a young man. It wasn't right at all.

Yet, the pull he felt was undeniable. Was this some strange form of flattery, a response to his brilliance? Or was there something more, something William couldn't—or wouldn't—bring himself to admit?

He growled, the sound echoing through the quiet office corridors as they walked.

This was madness. He needed a clear head. A plan. Anything.

The imposing oak doors of Monsieur Rousseau's office swung open with a heavy sigh, revealing a vision of polished mahogany and gleaming brass.

A young man with severe tan skin and an even sharper expression stood behind a gleaming desk.

"Monsieur William? And …" He trailed off, his gaze flickering to Louis with a hint of surprise before settling back on William. His tone was clipped. "Your … assistant, I presume?"

The word "assistant" hung in the air, a subtle barb aimed at Louis. William swallowed his irritation.

"Yes," he said, forcing a smile. "This is Louis. We have an appointment with Monsieur Rousseau."

The man's eyebrows shot up. "Monsieur Rousseau is currently in a meeting," he announced. "He won't be interrupted. Please, take a seat in the waiting room."

He gestured towards a doorway at the far end of the opulent reception area. William exchanged a helpless glance with Louis.

"How long will the meeting be?" Louis asked, his voice laced with a hint of impatience that mirrored William's frustration.

"It's impossible to say, Monsieur."

William sighed inwardly. Here, he wasn't an earl, but a businessman. He couldn't be authoritative.

An hour later, the plush waiting room felt more like a gilded cage. The air hung thick with the scent of expensive cigars and polished wood. Louis, perched on the edge of a pristine white armchair, seemed to shrink under the weight of the opulent surroundings.

"This is ridiculous," he muttered, tapping his foot impatiently. "How long does a meeting even take?"

William forced a smile. "Patience, Louis. Monsieur Rousseau seems to be a busy man."

Louis scoffed. "Busy or just making us wait to show off his power? Sounds like a typical business tactic to me."

William chuckled. "Perhaps," he conceded, "but it's a game we have to play, wouldn't you agree?"

Louis's gaze flickered up, his eyes meeting William's. The defiance that usually burned within them had softened, replaced by a flicker of something William couldn't decipher.

"Depends," Louis said, his voice a low murmur. "Is this a game you enjoy playing, Mr. William?"

The question hung in the air, heavy with unspoken meaning. William felt his heart skip a beat. He looked away, the air in the room suddenly stifling.

"Business is business, Louis," he said, his voice gruffer than intended.

A wry smile played on Louis's lips. "So it is," he agreed, the amusement in his voice sending a shiver down William's spine.

They lapsed into silence again, the weight of the unspoken hanging heavy between them. William stole a glance at Louis, his eyes drawn to the sharp line of his jaw, the way his throat worked as he swallowed. Louis' worn shirt did little to hide the subtle rise and fall of his chest.

He cleared his throat, the sound loud in the oppressive silence. "Louis," he began, his voice low and hesitant, "about before ..."

Before he could finish his thought, the door to the waiting room swung open.

The stern-faced assistant with the severe tan stood before them. "Monsieur Rousseau will see you now," he announced in a clipped French accent.

Relief washed over William, a wave so strong it almost knocked him off balance. He needed a distraction, anything to break the spell Louis had cast on him. He needed answers, and Monsieur Rousseau's meeting couldn't have come at a better time.

William stood, offering Louis a formal gesture towards the door. "Shall we?"

Chapter 9: Louisa

The rhythmic clatter of carriage wheels on cobblestones did little to soothe the knot of anxiety in Louisa's stomach. The business meeting in London had been a success, William's proposal securing the contract with his new business partner.

Relief should have washed over her, yet a cold dread gnawed at her insides.

They were near the outskirts of Havenwood when the carriage lurched to a sudden halt.

Louisa jolted upright, her heart hammering against her ribs. William, ever the composed gentleman, lowered the window a crack.

"What seems to be the problem?" he inquired, his voice calm yet firm.

A coarse-looking man with a scraggly beard leaned against the carriage door, his gaze sweeping over them both. "Just a routine check, gentlemen," he drawled, his voice laced with a dangerous edge. "Looking for a young woman, heiress to a tidy fortune, if you know what I mean."

Louisa's blood ran cold.

Heiress? Was this some elaborate ploy by Lord Blackwood to capture her?

Panic clawed at her throat, threatening to choke her. She had to get out of there. Now.

A quick glance at William revealed a frown creasing his brow. Confusion flickered in his eyes, quickly replaced by a steely determination.

"There are no ladies here," he stated, his voice firm. "Only myself and my... apprentice."

Apprentice.

The word scraped against Louisa's raw nerves. She wanted to scream, to reveal the truth about who she truly was. But a sliver of reason held her back.

She didn't understand William's motives yet. Was he protecting her, or simply playing along with some twisted game?

The bearded man sneered, his gaze lingering on Louisa for a beat too long. "Apprentice, eh? Looks a bit ... well-developed for a lad, wouldn't you say?" He reached out a grimy hand, aiming to yank open the carriage door.

Louisa flinched, instinctively recoiling.

William reacted with lightning speed. He grabbed the man's wrist, his grip surprisingly strong.

"I said there will be no search," he growled, his voice laced with a dangerous edge that sent sensation down Louisa's spine. "This is Lord Blackwood's carriage, and I suggest you show some respect."

The mention of the title seemed to give the man pause. He hesitated, his eyes darting from William's steely gaze to Louisa's pale face.

A tense silence stretched between them, broken only by the nervous snorting of the horses.

Finally, the leader of the hooligans grunted in what could be construed as an apology. "Apologies, Lord Blackwood. We were misinformed. Carry on."

"Wait!" A very familiar voice called out and Louisa almost fainted from the intensity of the voice.

It was him. Lord Thorne.

The very man who had orchestrated her downfall. The man who had hunted her like prey.

Shivers wracked her body, a primal fear clawing at her throat.

Instinct took over, urging her to shrink back into the shadows of the carriage, to disappear completely.

William noticed and his face contorted in a frown, but he sighed in determination and turned towards the source of the voice, his expression unreadable.

"Lord Thorne," William acknowledged, a hint of annoyance creeping into his voice. "What brings you to the outskirts of Havenwood?"

Louisa peeked through the gap in the curtains, her heart hammering against her ribs. Lord Thorne, mounted on a sleek black stallion, stood a few paces away, his face a mask of cold amusement.

"Just a bit of... unfinished business," he drawled, his gaze lingering pointedly on the carriage. "I believe a certain runaway heiress might be hiding in there."

Louisa's blood ran cold. He knew. Somehow, he had discovered her whereabouts.

Panic threatened to consume her, but a surge of defiance choked it back.

No, she wouldn't crumble.

Not in front of William.

Not in front of this snake, Thorne.

"Like I've told your ... men," William's voice cut through the oppressive silence, his words laced with a steely resolve Louisa hadn't heard before, "there is no heiress in my carriage, and there won't be a search."

Lord Thorne, for the first time since his arrival, seemed surprised.

His amusement faltered momentarily, replaced by a flicker of something resembling suspicion in his eyes. He scanned the carriage, his gaze lingering pointedly on the tightly drawn curtains.

"Very well, Blackwood," he finally conceded, a sly smile playing on his lips.

The smile sent a fresh wave of nausea churning in Louisa's stomach.

It was a smile that promised trouble, a reminder of the ruthless man beneath the veneer of charm.

"Perhaps we've been misinformed," Thorne continued, his voice laced with a dangerous smoothness. "My apologies for the inconvenience."

He cast another lingering glance at the carriage, his eyes seemingly boring into Louisa's hiding place.

Then, with a curt nod that felt more like a threat, he turned his horse and barked a command to his men.

Louisa held her breath as the clatter of hooves grew fainter, their pursuers finally disappearing into the gathering twilight. Only then did she dare to release the breath she hadn't realized she was holding.

Exhaustion washed over her, a heavy cloak settling on her already weary shoulders.

Lord Thorne might have conceded for the time being, but Louisa knew this wasn't over. He wouldn't give up so easily. He was a relentless predator, and she was his prey.

A glance at William revealed him staring out the window, his face etched with a grim determination.

There was a new layer to him now, a fierceness that surprised her.

He had stood up to Thorne, a powerful man with considerable influence, to protect her.

The realization sent a strange warmth blooming in her chest, quickly doused by a cold wave of logic.

Gratitude wasn't enough. She couldn't afford to let her emotions cloud her judgment.

William was still an enigma, a mystery wrapped in an Earl's cloak.

Chapter 10: William

The carriage clattered along the cobblestone streets, the rhythmic clip-clop of the horses' hooves the only sound that dared break the tense silence hanging heavy in the air.

Goodness.

William stole a glance at Louis, who sat stiffly in the corner, his face pale and drawn.

Gone was the fiery spirit that had propelled him through the meeting with the French businessman, replaced by a quiet fragility that tugged at something deep within William.

A lot of things had changed since the meeting.

He fought a war within himself. A part of him—a part he couldn't quite define—yearned to reach out, to offer Louis some form of comfort.

The urge to touch him, to soothe the tremors wracking his slender frame, was a sensation entirely foreign to William.

He'd always prided himself on his stoicism, his ability to navigate the world with a stiff upper lip and a firm hand.

Yet, here he was, his composure shaken by the sight of a young man, a mere boy by appearances, crumbling before him.

The revelation startled him. Since Louis's unexpected arrival weeks ago, William had been a whirlwind of confused emotions.

The initial annoyance at his jumpy presence had quickly morphed into begrudging respect, then something more.

The way Louis's eyes lit up with passion during a debate, the way his voice dropped to a soft husky whisper during their heated arguments—each interaction had chipped away at William's carefully constructed walls, exposing a vulnerability he hadn't known existed.

But what did it all mean?

He felt a strong sense of protection anytime it came to the boy and his well-being.

The image of Louis's trembling hands when confronted by Lord Thorne flashed in his mind.

The mention of Lady Louisa, a name that had elicited such a visceral reaction from Louis, sent another jolt through William.

There was more to Louis than met the eye, a hidden story veiled in fear and uncertainty.

Was Louis somehow connected to Lady Louisa? Was that the secret he clung to so desperately?

The possibility ignited a spark of curiosity within William. He craved answers. He just didn't know how to go about getting them.

William cleared his throat, the sound echoing awkwardly in the enclosed space. "Louis," he began, his voice gruff, "are you alright?"

Louis flinched at the sound, his head snapping up to meet William's gaze. His eyes, usually sparkling with defiance, were clouded with a deep-seated fear.

For a moment, William saw a young woman, lost and alone, a stark contrast to the brash facade Louis presented to the world. The image pierced him to the core, a strange protectiveness welling up within him.

But William shook the thought off. It was absurd, his thoughts. Louis was anything but a woman.

"I... I'm fine," Louis stammered, his voice barely a whisper.

William knew it was a lie. But something held him back from pressing the issue. Perhaps it was the fear mirrored in Louis's eyes, a fear that resonated with a secret loneliness of his own.

With a sigh, William settled back against the plush seat, his gaze fixed on the passing scenery.

The silence settled back in, thick and heavy. However, this time, it wasn't a void, but a promise.

A silent vow William made to himself, a vow to unravel the mystery that was Louis. He wouldn't let this go. He would find the truth, whatever it may be, and in doing so, perhaps he would also find answers to the unsettling questions stirring within his own heart.

***

The carriage rattled to a halt outside the bookstore, the sound a jarring interruption to the tense silence that had dominated the ride home.

Louis, still a pale ghost of his former self, shifted in the corner of the carriage, absent minded.

"Here we are," William announced, his voice gruff.

Relief flickered across Louis's face, a fleeting emotion quickly replaced by something akin to ... fear?

William frowned, the memory of Louis's reaction to Lord Thorne returning to haunt him.

"Would you like me to walk you to the door?" William offered, surprised by the words leaving his lips.

Louis had always struck him as fiercely independent, but the vulnerability etched on his face demanded some form of reassurance.

Louis hesitated for a moment, then nodded curtly. As William climbed down from the carriage, he couldn't help but notice the way Louis's hand trembled as he reached for the door handle. Again, without thinking, William offered his own hand in silent support.

The touch sent a jolt through William. Louis's hand, surprisingly small and slender, was encased in a worn leather glove, but even through the barrier, William could feel the delicacy of the bones beneath. It was a sensation that echoed the memory of his brief hold on Louis in the waiting room, a fleeting touch that had ignited a firestorm within him.

Their eyes met, and for a heartbeat, the world around them seemed to fade away.

The silence stretched, thick with unspoken emotions. William longed to bridge the gap, to understand the fear that lurked beneath the surface of Louis's brave exterior. He cleared his throat, the sound breaking the spell.

"About Lord Thorne," William began, his voice low, "and the mention of Lady Louisa, why were you so scared?"

Louis flinched visibly, his eyes darting away from William's gaze. "I ... I don't know," he stammered, a hint of desperation creeping into his voice. "Lord Thorne, it seems, has a rather unpleasant aura to his being, and it scared me a little."

The lie was palpable, as flimsy as moth-eaten tapestry. But something in Louis's demeanor, a raw vulnerability that tugged at William's protective instincts, stopped him from pushing further.

"Very well," William said finally, his voice devoid of judgment. "If you wish to speak of it, my door is always open." He squeezed Louis's hand gently before releasing it.

Louis mumbled a thanks, his voice barely above a whisper. Then, with a final lingering glance, disappeared into the bookstore.

William watched him go, a myriad of emotions churning within him. Louis was a puzzle wrapped in an enigma. The fear he'd displayed at the mention of Lady Louisa, the delicate touch of his hand—all of it pointed towards a hidden past, a secret Louis desperately guarded.

And for the first time, William realized the truth. He wasn't just determined to secure the cocoa bean deal. He was determined to unravel the mystery that was Louis.

The truth, whatever it may be, lay buried beneath layers of lies and fear. And William, with a tenacity born of both curiosity and a burgeoning protective instinct, wouldn't rest until he unearthed it.

He stalked back to the carriage. "Let's go home," he ordered, and throughout the ride, his thoughts were filled with Louis.

Minutes later, William dismissed the carriage, unease settling in his stomach as he approached his doorstep. It wasn't the prospect of another evening spent within the confines of his quiet home that caused the disquiet. No, it was the sight that greeted him on the steps— a sight as unexpected as a snowstorm in July.

There, perched primly on the wicker bench, sat his mother, Lady .

Her usually impeccably coiffed auburn hair was slightly askew, a testament to the haste of her journey, and her perfectly tailored gown seemed a touch out of place amongst the muted tones of his rural residence.

"Mother?" William frowned, surprise lacing his voice. He hadn't seen her in months, not since his last obligatory visit to London.

Lady Beth rose, her lips pressed into a thin line. "Son," she acknowledged, her voice laced with a cool formality that sent a shiver down his spine. "It seems necessary for us to have a ... conversation."

William swallowed the knot that had formed in his throat. Conversations with his mother, especially unplanned ones, rarely boded well. "Of course, Mother," he said, ushering her inside.

The calming scent of lavender and beeswax polish greeted them as they entered the house. A fire crackled in the hearth, casting a warm glow on the meticulously kept parlor, a stark contrast to the bohemian chaos William had allowed to flourish in his London shop.

His mother, however, seemed unimpressed by the cozy ambiance. Her gaze swept around the room, landing on a pile of well-worn books stacked precariously on a chair.

"William." She sighed, a sound that spoke volumes of her disapproval. "One would think you were running a literary den rather than a respectable home. You said to me in your letter that you were living well here. This does not look like living well, son."

William held back a groan. His mother's obsession with appearances was a constant source of tension between them. Here, amongst the rolling hills and quaint villages, he could finally shed the suffocating persona London society demanded. But his mother, it seemed, wasn't about to let him have his peace.

He forced a smile. "I am living well, mother. In fact, I find this place rather conducive to quiet contemplation."

Lady Beatrice sniffed. "Contemplation or eccentricity, the result seems the same." She paused, her eyes narrowing. "But that is not the reason for my visit."

William's heart sank. He knew that tone of voice. It was the prelude to an unpleasant revelation, a judgment delivered with the precision of a well-honed blade.

"Then what brings you here, Mother?" he asked, already dreading the answer.

"News travels fast, even to this remote corner of the world," Lady Beatrice said, her voice clipped. "Whispers have reached my ears regarding your unconventional business arrangements."

William felt a surge of irritation. It was bad enough that gossip circulated in London about the new, unconventional bookseller. He hadn't expected the rumors to spread so fast from his secluded haven. "Unconventional arrangements?" he repeated, his voice tight.

"Don't play coy, William," his mother said, her voice sharp. "I've heard tales about a young apprentice you've taken on. A rather unorthodox choice, wouldn't you say?"

William's blood ran cold. *Louis.*

His mother had heard about Louis. The thought of his friendship, the strange and unexpected connection they shared, being dissected by London's elite sent a wave of anger through him.

Anyone but Louis!

"So what?" he blurted out, unable to contain his frustration. "Louis is a valuable asset to the bookstore. He's intelligent, well-read, and ..." he hesitated, unsure of how to articulate the way Louis challenged him, pushed him in ways no one else ever had.

Lady Beatrice's eyes widened in shock. "William!" she exclaimed, her voice laced with a mixture of horror and disappointment. "Such familiarity! You cannot allow society to misunderstand you."

William gritted his teeth. "Misunderstand me? I'm running a business, Mother! Not conducting a courtship with a boy!"

"Business or not," his mother retorted, her voice regaining its icy composure, "appearances matter, William. You cannot simply defy societal norms without consequence. Think of your reputation. Your standing!"

William stared at her, his jaw clenched. The stifling expectations, the constant need to maintain a certain image—that was the life he had left behind in London. He wouldn't let his mother drag it back into his quiet existence, especially not when it came to Louis.

"My reputation," he said finally, his voice low and dangerous, "is of no concern to me as long as my business prospers. And as for Louis," he added, meeting his mother's disapproving gaze, "he's simply an employee. A talented one at that. Nothing more."

The words, even to his ears, tasted bitter. Yet, the thought of his mother dissecting his friendship with Louis, of using them as another weapon in her arsenal of societal control, was unbearable.

Lady Beatrice studied him for a long moment, her sharp eyes searching his face for any hint of deception. Finally, she seemed to accept, for now, his explanation.

"Very well," she said, her voice laced with a hint of resignation. "But remember, William," she continued, her words dripping with icy condescension, "even in the quietest corners of the world, appearances matter. Don't give the gossipmongers of London any ammunition."

"I don't care for London or its society."

William offered a tight smile, knowing full well that the conversation was far from over.

The silence that followed his declaration hung heavy in the air, thicker even than his mother's disapproval. William watched as Lady Beatrice straightened her silk gown, her movements deliberate, each rustle a testament to her displeasure.

"Very well, William," she said finally, her voice laced with a steely resolve. "If this is the path you choose to tread, then I suppose I have no choice but to adjust my schedule."

William's brow furrowed. "Adjust your schedule?"

Lady Beatrice offered a steely smile that didn't reach her eyes. "Indeed. It seems a visit of a longer duration is necessary. To ensure, shall we say, that appearances remain ... unblemished."

His frustration bubbled over. "Mother, this is absurd! You can't simply stay here indefinitely, dictating my business affairs."

"Indefinitely? Perhaps not," she said, "but long enough to ensure that the good people of this town understand the unique nature of your partnership with your ... apprentice is nothing more than what it is."

William gritted his teeth. The very notion of his mother gossiping about his affairs with the townsfolk was enough to make his skin crawl. "Mother, please," he started to protest, "there is no—"

"No scandal. I understand," she cut him off, her voice dripping with sarcasm. "But, William, a gentleman does not hire or provide living quarters to a young, unmarried male, especially one of questionable background."

The sting of her words was sharp. Louis's past, whatever it may be, wasn't a stain to be erased. It was a part of him ... but it also was something William was determined to understand, not exploit.

"Louis is a valuable asset to the business," he muttered through his teeth. "I said this before. His knowledge and intellect far surpass those of any other potential employee."

Lady Beatrice scoffed. "Knowledge and intellect are admirable qualities, William, but they cannot erase societal norms. A bookshop may be your haven, but the world outside its walls operates by different rules."

"Then perhaps," William said finally, his voice low and dangerous, "it's time I redefined those rules."

Lady Beatrice's eyes narrowed. "William, defiance is a dangerous game to play," she warned, her voice laced with a dangerous edge, "especially for someone with your title and a budding business to nurture."

"Then so be it, Mother," he said, his voice firm. "I will not apologize for my choices, nor will I allow you to dictate them."

A tense silence stretched between them, charged with unspoken emotions. Finally, Lady Beatrice sighed, a sound of weary acceptance.

With that, she swept towards the door, her silk gown whispering against the wooden floorboards. "I shall retire for now," she announced, her voice echoing through the room. "We shall discuss this further during dinner."

She disappeared into the grand estate, leaving William filled with frustration.

***

Should I go for dinner, or must I starve myself for the night? William asked himself for the millionth time.

The tension of the afternoon lingered like a fog as he slowly descended the stairs for a late supper.

He hoped for the solace of a quiet meal, a chance to gather his thoughts before facing his mother again in the morning.

But the moment he stepped into the dining room, hope disappeared like steam from a hot cup of tea.

Seated across from his mother, a woman he didn't recognize was sipping from a delicate porcelain cup. Her back was to him, but her posture spoke volumes—straight as a ramrod and radiating a cool composure that perfectly mirrored his mother's.

He cleared his throat, drawing their attention.

Lady Beatrice turned, a practiced smile gracing her lips. "Ah, son! There you are. Perfect timing."

The woman turned as well. Her face was framed by a cascade of blonde curls the color of a waterfall in sunlight. Her eyes, a soft brown, met his gaze with a flicker of surprise that quickly morphed into cool appraisal.

She possessed the kind of classic beauty that men wanted.

Not him though.

"William," Lady Beatrice announced, her voice laced with a hint of forced cheer, "allow me to introduce you to Lady Jacqueline Kensington."

The name made William's back stiffen. The Kensingtons were an influential family, their wealth and social standing unmatched except by his.

He recalled whispers from his youth about a potential alliance between the two families, but those were quickly silenced when he expressed his opposition to arranged marriages.

So, what now?

Lady Jacqueline stood and curtsied beautifully, her coy smile grating on his nerves. "My Lord," she greeted.

"Lady Jacqueline," he replied, his voice betraying none of the anger churning within him.

It was obvious his mother was playing matchmaker again.

Lady Beatrice, seemingly oblivious to the undercurrents swirling around them, beamed with delight. "I thought it would be delightful for you two to get acquainted," she said, her voice dripping with forced enthusiasm. "Lady Jacqueline has graciously agreed to stay for a few days. Perhaps a picnic in the garden is in order?"

The suggestion felt suffocating. A picnic with his mother and a potential marriage prospect—the very notion made him want to throw up.

"A delightful idea, Lady Beatrice," Lady Jacqueline said.

William forced a smile, the taste of ash in his mouth. Dinner would soon be over, he told himself. He could retreat to his study and forget this nightmare.

Was this his mother's solution to his "unconventional" arrangement with Louis? A calculated attempt to steer him back into the "proper" social circles, a gilded cage far more suffocating than the confines of his quiet life?

The night had taken an unexpected turn, and William had no idea how to escape it.

Chapter 11: Louisa

Oh, but he is so handsome.

Louisa meticulously dusted a beautifully illuminated manuscript, a faint blush creeping up her neck.

The document, a collection of chivalric romances, was a far cry from the ledgers and account books she was used to, but she threw herself into the task with efficiency.

Her mind, however, was far from the delicate parchment and vibrant illustrations.

It was replaying the scene from earlier that day, the memory of William standing up to Lord Thorne sending a jolt through her.

The fear, the raw panic, had been momentarily overshadowed by a surge of something else.

Gratitude? Perhaps.

But it was quickly choked by the ever-present awareness of her precarious situation.

He had protected her, yes, but for what reason? Was it simply a matter of principle as he'd claimed, or was there more to it?

A sigh escaped her lips, a wisp of air that carried the lingering scent of lavender and something distinctly masculine—a phantom echo of William that sent a shiver down her spine.

No.

She wouldn't allow herself to dwell on such things.

He was an earl, a man of privilege and power. She, on the other hand, was a fugitive, a ghost living on borrowed time.

A creak of the shop door pulled her back to reality. An elderly woman with kind eyes and a silver braid wound around her head peered inside.

"Good morning, young man," she greeted, her voice laced with a gentle curiosity. "Haven't seen you here before."

Louisa plastered on a smile, pushing down the familiar ache in her chest that accompanied this charade. "Good morning, Madam. I'm the new apprentice, Louis. Welcome to Havenwood Books."

"Ah, an apprentice, are we?" The woman's gaze swept over Louisa's threadbare clothing and dusty cap. "Quite an adventurous choice for a young man."

Louisa shrugged, forcing a light tone. "Adventure is good for the soul, wouldn't you say?"

The woman chuckled, a warm sound that filled the shop. "Indeed, it is. I'm looking for something specific, if you wouldn't mind helping me."

Relief washed over Louisa.

Focusing on the customer was a welcome distraction from her inner turmoil. She spent the next few minutes conversing with the woman, her knowledge of literature coming to the fore.

Together, they searched the shelves, discussing different editions and authors with a shared enthusiasm that temporarily banished the shadows lurking in her mind.

Finally, they found the book the woman was looking for. As Louisa wrapped it up, the woman's gaze lingered on her.

"You know," she said, her voice soft, "there's a sadness in your eyes, young man. Like a story waiting to be told."

Louisa froze, her breath catching in her throat.

How could this woman see through her carefully constructed facade?

Panic clawed at her, the constant fear of discovery rearing its ugly head.

"I... I don't know what you mean, madam," she stammered, her voice barely a whisper.

The woman smiled sadly. "Perhaps not. But sometimes, keeping things bottled up only makes them heavier. If you ever need someone to talk to, look around you. I'm sure there are people willing to listen and understand you."

Before Louisa could respond, the bell above the door chimed, signaling the arrival of another customer. With a grateful smile, the woman excused herself and headed out.

Louisa stood there for a long moment, the woman's words echoing in her head.

A listening ear?

The very thought was tempting, a flicker of hope battling against the ever-present fear.

Could she confide in William? Could she trust him?

The memory of his steely gaze as he faced down Lord Thorne offered some reassurance.

But then a throat cleared behind her, sharp and sudden, shattering the fragile bubble of hope.

Louisa whirled around, heart leaping into her throat.

The world seemed to tilt on its axis, the air sucked from her lungs.

Standing there, amidst the towering shelves, was Lord Thorne.

For a moment, all thought fled.

The blood drained from her face, replaced by a cold dread that froze her limbs.

He had found her.

Here, in William's bookstore of all places.

Panic clawed at her throat, threatening to choke her.

Thorne, oblivious to her inner turmoil, strolled into the shop, his gaze sweeping the room with a predatory nonchalance. His polished boots echoed on the wooden floor as he approached her.

He was clad in his usual finery, a predatory smile playing on his lips.

His gaze, cold and calculating, swept over her, taking in her threadbare clothes and nervous posture.

It was a predator sizing up its prey, and Louisa felt a primal fear grip her.

"Well, well, well," he drawled, his voice dripping with amusement. "What do we have here? Havenwood's newest acquisition, I presume?"

Louisa's voice seemed to catch in her throat. "L-Lord Thorne," she stammered, forcing a smile that felt more like a grimace. "What a ... surprise."

He chuckled, his eyes glinting with a dangerous light. "Surprise indeed."

Louisa gritted her teeth and calmed herself as she spoke. "What ... what brings you here?" she finally managed, the words raspy and strained.

"A thirst for knowledge, of course," he replied, his gaze lingering on her a beat too long. "And perhaps a particular manuscript that piqued my interest."

He cast a sweeping glance around the shelves, his eyes lingering on the more valuable items.

Louisa knew it was a lie; a mere ploy to keep her on edge.

He wasn't here for books.

He was here for her.

"We have a wide selection of manuscripts," she managed, her voice regaining some semblance of control. "Perhaps you could tell me what you're looking for?"

Thorne chuckled, a low sound that sent goosebumps erupting on her skin. "Now, where's the fun in that?" he purred, his eyes narrowing. "I much prefer ... the thrill of the hunt."

His words sent a fresh wave of terror through her. He was toying with her, enjoying her fear. But Louisa, never one to back down from a fight, refused to crumble.

She was about to speak when he said, "I wasn't expecting to find a runaway heiress working in a dusty bookstore."

His words were a thinly veiled threat that sent a shiver down Louisa's spine.

He knew.

Somehow, he had discovered her whereabouts.

Panic clawed at her, but weeks of living a lie had honed her survival instincts.

Mustering a playful tone, she scoffed. "Runaway heiress? Whatever do you mean, Lord Thorne? I thought my master already cleared this up. I'm not the heiress you seek. I am just a young librarian boy trying to make a living."

The lie felt heavy on her tongue, a bitter pill to swallow. But it was the only weapon she had at the moment.

Lord Thorne's smile faltered for a moment, suspicion replacing the amusement in his eyes.

It was a subtle shift, almost imperceptible, but Louisa caught it. He was thrown off balance, at least momentarily. Perhaps her charade had some merit.

He ran his gaze over her threadbare clothes and nervous posture. "An apprentice, you say?" He leaned closer, his voice dropping to a low murmur. "One with such ... interesting knowledge of rare manuscripts?"

Louisa held his gaze, her own eyes hardening. "Perhaps this bookstore boasts a more extensive collection than you initially thought, Lord Thorne." She emphasized the last word, a subtle jab at his arrogance.

A muscle ticked in his jaw, betraying his annoyance. But he quickly recovered, a predatory smile returning to his lips.

"Perhaps," he conceded, his voice taking on a smooth, almost seductive tone. "But tell me, apprentice, do you always dust manuscripts with such fervor?" His gaze dropped pointedly to the way her hand lingered on the ancient parchment, a tremor barely contained within.

Louisa gritted her teeth, forcing her hand away. "One must take care of their inventory, wouldn't you agree?" she countered, her voice laced with sharp sarcasm.

Thorne chuckled again, the sound devoid of humor. He was toying with her, enjoying her discomfort. But Louisa wouldn't give him the satisfaction of seeing her crumble.

He sauntered around the shop, seemingly browsing the shelves but never taking his eyes off her.

He picked up a book here, a scroll there, all the while peppering her with questions about their origin, their value, their history.

With each question, Louisa felt the net tightening around her. She answered cautiously, weaving an intricate tapestry of lies, hoping it would be enough to throw him off guard. But beneath his feigned nonchalance, she sensed he was poking at her armor, looking for a weakness to exploit.

"Fascinating," he drawled, picking up a leather-bound volume filled with intricate botanical illustrations. He flipped through the pages with a practiced ease, his eyes narrowed as if searching for something specific. "Tell me, apprentice, do you know anything about ... hidden compartments?"

Louisa's breath hitched.

Hidden compartments?

Was he onto her secret hiding place, the one where she kept her most valuable possession—the locket containing her identity? Fear choked her, a cold dread radiating from her core.

Fear.

It was a dangerous emotion, a weakness she couldn't afford to show.

Straightening her spine, she forced a nervous laugh.

"Hidden compartments?" she stammered, her voice pitched a touch higher than usual. "Goodness, Lord Thorne, this shop is filled with history. Who knows what secrets these old books might hold? Perhaps hidden maps to buried treasure, or love letters from a bygone era." She winked, hoping to deflect his suspicion with a touch of theatricality.

Thorne's smile didn't reach his eyes.

He closed the book with a snap, his gaze locking onto hers.

There was a dangerous glint in his eyes.

Sweat droplets pooled on Louisa's forehead.

He was close. Too close.

She had to divert his attention; anything to throw him off the scent.

Her gaze darted around the shop, scanning for a weapon, or an escape route—anything.

Suddenly, a bell above the shop door chimed, the sweet melody a lifeline in the suffocating tension. Louisa spun around, a theatrical smile plastered on her face.

"Ah! A customer!" she exclaimed, her voice a touch too loud. "Excuse me, Lord Thorne, but duty calls."

Before Thorne could respond, she practically skipped towards the door, her mind racing.

Entering the shop was Mr. Abernathy, and as soon as he saw Lord Thorne he frowned and looked at Louisa, then quickly stepped in between them.

"Lord Thorne," Mr. Abernathy greeted, his voice laced with a polite formality. "What a surprise to see you here."

Thorne, momentarily thrown off guard, straightened up. "Abernathy," he acknowledged with a curt nod. "Just browsing your ... eclectic selection."

"Indeed, indeed." Mr. Abernathy chuckled, his gaze lingering on Louisa. "Our new apprentice, Louis, is quite knowledgeable."

Louisa plastered a grateful smile on her face. Mr. Abernathy's arrival was a godsend, a shield against Lord Thorne's predatory gaze.

"So, it seems," Thorne drawled, his eyes narrowing as they met Louisa's. "Well, Abernathy, I wouldn't want to keep you from your business." He emphasized the last word, a thinly veiled threat.

"Of course, Lord Thorne," Mr. Abernathy replied, ushering him towards the door. "Do come again."

With a curt nod and a lingering glance at Louisa, Lord Thorne swept out of the shop.

The second the door closed behind him, the air seemed to crackle with tension.

Mr. Abernathy turned to Louisa, his kind eyes filled with concern. "Louis, are you alright? That seemed a rather ... tense exchange."

The adrenaline that had fueled her bravado ebbed away, leaving behind a wave of exhaustion and fear. Tears welled up in her eyes, blurring her vision.

"Mr. Abernathy," she choked out, voice thick with emotion. "I ... I can't take it anymore."

The older gentleman rushed to her side, placing a gentle hand on her shoulder. "Calm down, Louis. Calm down. Tell me what's wrong."

The words wouldn't come. Shame and fear battled for dominance, leaving her throat constricted, her voice stolen.

Seeing her distress, Mr. Abernathy ushered her towards a dusty armchair in the back corner of the shop. He fussed around her, bringing her a glass of water and a damp cloth.

"Here now." He patted her hand like he would a frightened child. "Take a few deep breaths. When you're ready, you can tell me what's troubling you."

Louisa closed her eyes, taking slow, shuddering breaths. The image of Lord Thorne's predatory smile flashed through her mind, a stark reminder of the danger she was in.

Finally, with a shaky voice, she began to speak.

The dam broke. Weeks of pent-up fear, anxiety, and loneliness came crashing down. Louisa, her voice choked with sobs, poured out her story. She spoke of her identity—Louisa, not Louis—a young woman forced to flee her aristocratic home to escape a forced marriage orchestrated by her greedy aunt.

She confessed her fear of being discovered, the constant threat of Lord Thorne looming over her. She spoke of the gnawing loneliness, and the yearning for a normal life, one where she wasn't constantly looking over her shoulder, living a lie.

Mr. Abernathy listened patiently, his kind eyes reflecting her pain.

When she finally finished, her voice hoarse and raw, a heavy silence descended upon the shop.

"Oh, my dear," Mr. Abernathy finally said, his voice thick with emotion. "I can't even begin to imagine what you've been through." He reached out and squeezed her hand gently. "Why didn't you tell me before? I may not be much, but I'm here for you."

Louisa looked up at him, her eyes brimming with tears. His simple words and his genuine concern were a balm to her wounded soul. Shame threatened to engulf her, but she pushed it down. She needed help, and Mr. Abernathy, with his kind heart and grandfatherly demeanor, was her only lifeline.

"I ... I was afraid," she confessed, her voice barely a whisper. "Afraid you wouldn't believe me ... that you'd turn me in."

Mr. Abernathy chuckled softly. "Turn you in? Never. You, my dear, are far braver than you give yourself credit for. Running away, taking charge of your own life ... that takes courage."

His words were a revelation. Louisa hadn't seen it that way before. She had been so focused on surviving, on keeping her secret, that she hadn't realized she had, in fact, displayed a strength she never knew she possessed.

"But you can't keep running forever," Mr. Abernathy continued, his voice firm yet gentle. "We need to come up with a plan."

A raw, ragged sob escaped her lips.

"There, there," Mr. Abernathy murmured, offering a comforting pat on the shoulder. "It's alright, child. You did what you had to do."

Louisa shook her head, tears still streaming down her face. "What am I going to do now, Mr. Abernathy? He'll find me. Lord Thorne ..."

The older gentleman squeezed her shoulder gently. "Let's not jump to conclusions, Louisa," he said, using her real name for the first time. "We'll figure something out. But for now, you need rest."

He helped her to her feet and led her to the small room she now called her own, then handed her a carafe of warm water and a book.

"Read if you can," he said kindly. "Or sleep. Whatever helps you relax."

Chapter 12: William

Sleep, despite his best efforts, eluded William that night. For reasons he wasn't sure he wanted to entertain, he tossed and turned in his bed, the silence of the mansion increasing the disquiet gnawing at him.

Finally, unable to bear the confines of his chamber any longer, William quickly threw on his clothes and descended the stairs.

The quiet hum of the expensive gaslight he had gotten from France offered a sliver of comfort, and he found himself drawn, almost unconsciously, to his bookstore.

It wasn't so late in the night, and the store would be open.

Will Louis be there? he wondered.

A few minutes later, he got off his horse and entered the bookstore. Bathed in the soft glow of a solitary lamp, it presented a picture of peaceful solitude.

Mr. Abernathy, perched on a stool tucked away in a corner, was engrossed in a leather-bound volume.

William looked around but didn't find any scuttling man.

"Mr. Abernathy," he called, his voice low.

The old man started, his spectacles slipping down his nose. A smile creased his wizened face once he recognized William.

"Ah, my lord! Unexpected pleasure to see you at this hour," he exclaimed, adjusting his spectacles. "Can't sleep, eh?"

William chuckled, a hollow sound in the stillness. "Something akin to that, Mr. Abernathy. Couldn't seem to settle my mind."

"So, you've come to see the new book arrival?"

"Yes." William looked around again. "Where is Louis?" he asked in a voice he hoped was not as intense as he felt.

Mr. Abernathy had a look in his eyes before he smiled. "The lad has retired for the night; he had a long day."

William tried not to look so disappointed as he scoffed. "He's getting lazy, that's what."

"Ah, the troubles of the young," Mr. Abernathy said with a wink. "But enough of that. You said you were looking for something. A particular book perhaps?"

William nodded and started to browse the shelves, running his fingers along the worn spines of countless books. The familiar scent of old paper and leather sparked a sense of calm within him, a temporary respite from the storm brewing inside.

"How was business today?" he asked finally, more to ease the silence than anything else.

Mr. Abernathy chuckled. "Lively, my lord, lively! We had quite the assortment of customers, all eager to delve into the new arrivals." He paused, concern flitting across his eyes. "Though, we did have a bit of an ... unpleasant encounter earlier."

William's brow furrowed. "Unpleasant?"

"Indeed," Mr. Abernathy confirmed, lowering his voice. "Lord Thorne was here earlier, and he tried to cause trouble for our Louis."

A jolt of shock ran through William. Lord Thorne again? Why would he come here looking for Louis? And what exactly did he want?

The questions pounded in William's head, a drumbeat of worry.

"Did he cause any trouble?" he asked, his voice tight with concern.

Mr. Abernathy shook his head. "Thankfully, no. I was able to salvage the situation."

William let out a breath he hadn't realized he was holding. Relief washed over him, intertwined with a surge of protectiveness towards Louis. The very idea of the young man being hounded by Lord Thorne sent a shiver down his spine.

"Did Louis say anything about Lord Thorne's visit?" he pressed, his curiosity gnawing at him.

Mr. Abernathy scratched his chin thoughtfully. "Not a word, though, he did seem a tad more ... flustered than usual after the encounter."

"Thank you, Mr. Abernathy," William said finally, his voice filled with gratitude. "For everything. I think I found what I need." He raised a book in the air.

The old man smiled warmly. "Think nothing of it. Sleep well," he added, a mischievous glint in his eye. "A good book is always the best remedy for a restless night."

Curiosity, a relentless gnawing beast, clawed at William's insides as he stepped back out onto the quiet street.

Lord Thorne's visit confirmed what he'd suspected for some time: Louis was not who he appeared to be. The fear that had flickered in Louis's eyes at the mere mention of the name, his reaction when Thorne's men had tried to search the carriage ... everything. It was suspicious.

A newfound determination solidified in his chest. He had to know more. He had to understand.

He retraced his steps back into the bookstore. Mr. Abernathy was now meticulously rearranging a shelf of travelogues.

"Mr. Abernathy," William began, his voice hesitant, "about Louis..."

The old man paused in mid-reach, his head snapping up to meet William's gaze. A flicker of something akin to alarm passed through his usually benevolent eyes.

"Yes, my lord?"

"Has anything about Louis struck you as ... odd?" William pressed, struggling to articulate the question churning in his mind.

Mr. Abernathy's brow furrowed, a tense silence settling between them. He scrutinized William for a long moment, his gaze filled with an unreadable emotion.

"Odd?" Mr. Abernathy finally echoed, his voice a low murmur. "Well, he is a bright young lad, that much is certain. Possesses a thirst for knowledge you don't often see in these parts."

William's frustration mounted. "Yes," he conceded, "but there's something else, isn't there? Something about his past, perhaps."

Mr. Abernathy's silence stretched on, thick with unspoken knowledge. Finally, he sighed, a deep, weary sound that spoke volumes.

"Sometimes," he began, his voice low and measured, "the past is best left undisturbed. Louis ... well, Louis has his burdens. It's not my story to tell."

A wall, invisible yet impenetrable, had risen between them. William understood the unspoken message: Mr. Abernathy wouldn't betray Louis's trust.

But the old man's words only fueled his curiosity further. What secret did Louis harbor? Why was Lord Thorne so intent on finding him?

"But Mr. Abernathy," William persisted, his voice laced with desperation, "doesn't Louis deserve a chance to explain himself? Doesn't he deserve a future free from whatever shadows his past holds?"

Mr. Abernathy met his gaze, a flicker of sadness passing through his eyes. "That, my lord," he said gently, "is entirely up to Louis. And perhaps, in time, he will choose to share his burden with you."

William felt a pang of disappointment. He yearned to understand Louis, to break down the walls the young man had erected around himself. Yet, Mr. Abernathy's words gave him a sliver of hope. Perhaps, in time, Louis would confide in him.

With a heavy heart, William turned to leave. "Thank you, Mr. Abernathy," he said, his voice quieter than a whisper. "Good night."

As he walked away, the weight of Mr. Abernathy's words pressed down on William. Louis was not who he seemed. His past was a tightly locked box, and the key lay solely with Louis himself.

The revelation sent a shiver down William's spine. He had let himself get so close to a young man shrouded in mystery. Was he being naive? Was he putting himself at risk by trusting someone with such a hidden past?

The doubts gnawed at him, but they were overshadowed by a deeper feeling—a protectiveness for Louis, a desire to see him free of whatever burdened him.

He had taken a leap of faith by offering Louis a job and a place to stay. Now, it seemed, he would have to take another - a leap of trust. He would wait, patiently and with unwavering support, for Louis to choose whether he wanted to share his truth.

***

William continued down the cobblestone path, his conversation with Mr. Abernathy still playing in his mind. The cool night air did little to soothe the turmoil within him.

He wandered aimlessly, the silvery light of the moon casting long shadows across the deserted streets. The gentle murmur of the nearby river provided a hypnotic soundtrack to his restless thoughts.

As he rounded a bend in the path, the sound of splashing water reached his ears. He hesitated, his heart skipping a beat. It was an uncharacteristically warm night for a late-night swim, but curiosity propelled him forward.

He crept closer, careful not to make a sound. The sight that greeted him sent a jolt of surprise through his system. A figure, silhouetted against the moonlit water, stood at the riverbank.

His initial shock quickly morphed into something akin to panic.

He understood the allure of a cool dip on a warm night, but the danger of being discovered, the potential scandal ...

He opened his mouth to call out, to warn the figure of their precarious position, when a sudden gust of wind tousled their hair, revealing its color.

The moonlight glinted off auburn curls, the same fiery shade that adorned Louis's head.

His breath hitched in his throat.

The image was so incongruous, so utterly unexpected, that it took him a moment to process the scene before him.

Then another burst of shock ripped through William like a bolt of lightning.

The cascading auburn hair, the figure bathed in the moonlight ... could it be?

Was Louis, the enigmatic young man he'd taken under his wing, the one he'd shared countless conversations with, the one who had stirred a strange sense of ... something within him, a woman?

A woman.

His mind reeled, struggling to reconcile the image before him with the confident, sharp-minded individual he knew. The world seemed to tilt on its axis, familiar landmarks dissolving into a blurry haze.

She, for it was undeniably a woman, now stood waist-deep in the water, her back turned to him. The air crackled with a tension that had nothing to do with the cool night breeze.

William knew he should turn away, respect her privacy and this astonishing revelation. Yet, his feet remained rooted to the spot.

He cleared his throat, the sound harsh in the quiet night. "Louis?" he called out.

At the sound of the name, she whirled around with a gasp, her eyes wide with alarm. The moonlight glinted off the water droplets clinging to her face, and for a fleeting moment, they both stood stock still.

It was, without a doubt, Louis.

Before he could say anything else, she turned and ducked under the water without a moment's hesitation, disappearing.

A heartbeat later, a ripple spread across the surface of the river, followed by a flash of movement as she emerged further down the bank, farther away from him.

And then she ran away.

William just stood there like a man who had seen a ghost.

A woman.

***

The ride back to his mansion was a blur. The revelation about Louis echoed in his mind, a discordant symphony of questions and confusion.

His steps felt heavy, burdened not just by the weight of this new truth but also by the unexpected emotions it unearthed.

She lied to him.

She was a woman.

She lied to him.

He finally arrived at the familiar threshold of his mansion, but instead of seeking sanctuary within the sheltering walls of his chamber, he found himself drawn to another room —his late wife's sanctuary.

Years had passed since Anna's passing, yet the room remained untouched, a monument to a love tragically cut short.

Soft moonlight streamed through the lace curtains, illuminating the space with a melancholic glow. Memories flooded in, bittersweet and poignant—stolen kisses in the twilight, Anna's gentle laughter echoing in the room, the dreams they had woven for their future.

He sank onto the plush chaise lounge, the worn velvet whispering his name like a long-forgotten melody. Their unborn child would have been five years old now. The thought of it, a beautiful phantom in his mind, brought a fresh wave of grief.

He closed his eyes, the image of Louis, bathed in moonlight by the river, superimposed on the memory of Anna's radiant smile.

Guilt, a constant companion for years, tightened its icy grip on his heart. How could he even entertain the notion of feelings for another woman, another soul, when he had failed to protect Anna and their child-to-be?

Everyone had said it wasn't his fault, that it was nature, but somehow, he felt that if he had been around ... if he hadn't been on that business trip, he would have noticed that his wife ran a very hot temperature, and he would have gotten a healer for her. It wouldn't have gotten so bad that she would have died in her sleep like that.

His marriage to Anna had been a love story whispered in soft glances and stolen touches. Their bond, though short-lived, had been as beautiful and fragile as a butterfly's wing.

He blamed himself for the tragic loss, the weight of that guilt a constant anchor in his life. He still did. How could he allow himself to be swept away by emotions that felt like a betrayal of her memory?

Yet, he couldn't stop thinking about what he had seen earlier that night.

He rose, his movements restless like a caged animal. He craved answers—not just about Louis, but about himself.

Did his feelings diminish the love he still held for Anna? Was it possible to honor his past while acknowledging the flicker of something new stirring within him?

What could he do?

Chapter 13: Louisa

The rising sun cast a golden glow across the room, painting long shadows on the dusty floorboards.

Louisa stirred awake, the events of the previous night replaying in her mind like a scene from a dream. The memory of someone's voice calling her name by the river sent a shiver down her spine.

It had been dark, so she hadn't seen who it was. It hadn't helped that they had been mostly hidden by trees.

Who was it?

Had they seen her? Had her secret been exposed in the moonlight's silvery gleam?

Restlessness gnawed at her.

She couldn't afford careless mistakes, not when her entire future hung in the balance.

Louisa quickly freshened up and opened the bookshop to get ready for the day's sale.

Just then, a gentle creaking of the shop door announced Mr. Abernathy's arrival. He bustled in, a cheerful smile plastered on his face.

"Good morning, Louis! Bright and early, I see."

Louisa forced a smile, the remnants of worry clinging to her like cobwebs. "Good morning, Mr. Abernathy. Did you sleep well?"

"Like a log," he boomed, bustling behind the counter. "Now, where did I put that new shipment of ..." He trailed off, his eyes landing on Louisa. The smile faded, replaced by concern. "You alright, Louis? You look a little pale."

Louisa touched her cheek, self-consciously. "Just a restless night, Mr. Abernathy. Nothing to worry about."

He peered at her with a fatherly concern that warmed her heart.

Mr. Abernathy, in his own way, had become a source of comfort and support during her lonely weeks here.

"Well, don't you fret," he said, his voice firm but kind. "Work always helps chase away the blues. Now, let's see what treasures we can unearth today."

As the day unfolded, filled with the familiar tasks of dusting books, helping customers, and losing herself in the comforting world of literature, Louisa couldn't shake the feeling that a decision loomed.

Mr. Abernathy's words, spoken during a lull in the afternoon rush, echoed in her mind.

"You know," he had said, his eyes twinkling with a knowing glint, "marriage might be the solution to your predicament."

Louisa had choked on her tea, sputtering in surprise. "Marriage? But Mr. Abernathy, I—"

He held up a hand, silencing her. "Hear me out," he said, his voice gentle. "A good husband —a respectable man—could provide you the protection you need. He could help you reclaim your inheritance from that wicked aunt of yours."

The idea had a certain appeal. It offered a path back to her rightful life, a way to escape the constant fear that gnawed at her.

A husband, a protector.

But who? She barely knew anyone here, and the thought of marrying a stranger was daunting.

Then, a face popped into her mind.

William, with his steely blue eyes and kind smile.

The thought sent a flutter through her stomach, a confusing mix of fear and hope.

He was strong, intelligent, and seemed to possess a sense of justice.

And there was no denying it: she found him extremely attractive.

Perhaps ... perhaps he could be the answer.

But what about his perception of her?

He knew her as Louis, the apprentice.

Would he even consider marrying a mere bookseller's assistant? And more importantly, could she trust him enough to let him in on her identity, the secret she had guarded so fiercely?

The knot of worry tightened in her stomach.

This wasn't a decision to be taken lightly.

But she knew one thing for certain—the longer she stayed hidden, the more precarious her situation would become.

Telling William the truth, as terrifying as it was, might be her only hope.

As the day ended and Mr. Abernathy locked the shop door, Louisa took a deep breath, a steely resolve forming in her heart.

Tonight, she would confide in William.

Tonight, she would tell him everything.

But first, she had a necessary task at hand.

The image of William seeing her disguised as a boy was enough to send a shiver down her spine.

No, she needed to approach him as Louisa, the woman she truly was.

"Mr. Abernathy," she began hesitantly as he flipped through a dusty ledger, "there's something I need your help with."

The old man looked up, his bushy eyebrows raised in concern. "What is it? And don't tell me you've lost that first folio of Shakespeare I entrusted you with."

Louisa chuckled, a genuine sound that surprised even her. "No, no, nothing like that. It's just ... I need to find some ... feminine attire."

Mr. Abernathy's eyes widened in surprise, then a slow smile spread across his face. "Ah, I see! Perhaps you've finally met a charming young lad, eh?"

Louisa felt a blush creep up her neck, but she held her ground. "Not exactly," she admitted. "There's just ... a situation. But I can't very well explain it if I look like a boy in borrowed clothes."

Mr. Abernathy's smile softened. "Of course, of course. Well, worry not. I have just the person in mind."

He rummaged through his desk drawer, emerging with a faded map and a mischievous glint in his eye. "My dear friend, Esme, runs a delightful little dress shop down by the harbor. Mention my name, and she'll take good care of you."

With the map clutched in her hand, Louisa felt a flicker of hope. Perhaps this was a good sign. Maybe revealing herself wouldn't be as daunting as she had initially feared.

The walk to the harbor was filled with nervous anticipation.

The map led her through winding streets, past bustling marketplaces, and finally to a quaint little shop tucked away in a quiet corner.

A bell tinkled as she pushed open the door, announcing her arrival.

The woman behind the counter looked up, her eyes widening in surprise as they landed on Louisa. She was older, with a warm smile and a kind twinkle in her eyes.

"Good day. Mr. Abernathy—"

"Mr. Abernathy sent you, did he?" she inquired, her voice a gentle melody.

Louisa nodded, suddenly feeling a little self-conscious. "He said you could help me ... find an outfit."

"Well, then you've come to the right place, dear!" Esme exclaimed, her enthusiasm infectious. "Tell me, what kind of look are you going for? Elegant? Playful? Perhaps a touch of mystery?"

Louisa, overwhelmed by the vibrant colors and shimmering fabrics that surrounded her, found herself blurting out her thoughts.

She described the image she wanted to project – confident, yet approachable, with a hint of her true strength hidden beneath.

Esme listened intently, nodding her head. Then, with a flourish, she began pulling out dresses from the racks, each one more stunning than the last.

For the next hour, Esme draped dresses of various styles on Louisa, offering advice and encouragement.

Louisa found herself laughing, twirling, and stepping out of her comfort zone.

It was the first time in weeks that she had allowed herself to simply be a woman, to revel in the feminine beauty she had kept hidden for so long.

Finally, Esme presented her final creation—a flowing gown of sapphire blue that hugged Louisa's curves in all the right places.

She had styled Louisa's hair, pulling it back in a way that accentuated her strong features yet retained a touch of elegance.

When Louisa looked in the mirror, she barely recognized herself. The woman staring back was no longer the scared boy she had portrayed.

She was Louisa, a woman of strength and resilience, ready to face her future.

"You look absolutely magnificent, dear!" Esme declared, clapping her hands in delight.

A wave of gratitude washed over Louisa. This kind, warm woman, with her infectious energy and genuine care, had done more than just offer her a dress. She had reminded Louisa of the woman she truly was —a woman worthy of love and respect.

After a heartfelt goodbye to Esme, Louisa returned to Havenwood, her heart pounding with a nervous anticipation.

Tonight, she would reveal herself to William, tell him everything, and hope beyond hope that he wouldn't be repulsed by her deception.

As she approached William's manor, the rising moon cast an ethereal glow on the grounds.

Taking a deep breath, she straightened her sapphire dress, the unfamiliar fabric whispering against her skin.

The Butler walked forward and looked at her skeptically. "Good evening, Miss. Who do you seek?"

She straightened her spine. "I seek the audience of Lord William."

The man's frown deepened. "And you are ..."

"Louisa," she answered. "I'm Louisa."

"Oh Louisa! I've heard about you from our lord." Then under his breath, "But the way the lord spoke, Louisa was supposed to be a man? Or has my hearing really gone bad?"

She froze and wished to all the heavens that she would be allowed in.

"Well, then, come in, my lady. I shall summon the lord for you," he said, and with a sigh of relief she followed him in.

He motioned for her to sit while he headed upstairs, but after a second or so, Louisa grew impatient, and her curiosity took the better of her.

She stood and went in the direction the Butler had gone.

And then she halted by a door tagged "study."

It had to be William's.

She neared and found the door slightly ajar, a sliver of warm light spilling out into the hallway. With a tremor in her hand, she pushed the door open, stepping tentatively inside.

The sight that greeted her froze the breath in her lungs.

William stood by the window, a woman with blonde hair clinging to his arm. Their faces were turned towards each other, the soft glow of the fireplace painting an intimate scene.

Louisa felt a cold dread pool in the pit of her stomach.

The woman, all smiles and playful banter, was gushing about some upcoming social event. William, a smile gracing his lips, was listening intently, his touch lingering a touch too long on the woman's arm.

Each word spoken felt like glass shattering around Louisa.

The man she had dreamt of confiding in, the man she'd dared to hope might offer her a safe haven, was already ... entangled.

The carefully constructed image of Louisa, the woman she intended to present to him, crumbled to dust.

What was the point anymore? Here she was, ready to lay her heart bare, and he was already taken. A bitter laugh escaped her lips, devoid of any humor.

The sound seemed to pierce through the oblivious couple's conversation.

William's head snapped up, his eyes widening in shock as he met Louisa's gaze.

Tears stung her eyes, blurring the world around her.

She didn't care where her feet took her as she hurried away. All she knew was that she needed to get away from the suffocating scene, away from the crushing disappointment that threatened to engulf her.

She pushed through the throng of servants walking down the hall, a human battering ram fueled by pure adrenaline.

She bumped into someone but didn't bother to turn back.

Suddenly, a bony hand clamped onto her arm, halting her escape. Louisa whipped around, ready to unleash a verbal tirade on whoever had dared to impede her flight, but the words died on her tongue.

Standing before her was an older woman who bore a striking resemblance to William.

"Who are you?" the woman barked, her voice a gravely rasp.

Louisa, momentarily stunned, simply stared.

This wasn't the time to be caught in a situation with a very angry woman, but something about the woman's fierce demeanor held her captive.

Louisa ripped her arm free, the fire returning to her eyes. "Not your concern, Lady," she spat, her voice tight but laced with the same kind of steel that glinted in the woman's narrowed gaze.

She didn't wait for a reply; she couldn't afford to. With a final, withering look, Louisa plunged back into the crowd, leaving the bewildered woman standing in her wake.

The cool night air whipped at her hair, carrying away the lingering scent of Esme's perfume and the bitter taste of betrayal.

She ran blindly, her sapphire dress catching on thorns and branches, a physical manifestation of the tangled mess her life had become.

Finally, exhausted, and emotionally drained, she stumbled to a halt, collapsing onto a park bench beneath a hulking oak tree.

The weight of her secret, the fear, the loneliness, all came crashing down on her in a wave of despair.

What was the point of it all?

She had given up everything—her home, her family, her life—for a sliver of hope, only to have it snatched away in the blink of an eye.

"Stupid Louisa," she muttered to herself, her voice thick with tears.

But amidst the self-pity and anger, defiance sparked within her.

No, she wouldn't let this break her.

She had faced worse and survived. Louisa Hastings was not a woman to be defined by rejection.

She wiped her tears with a shaky hand and straightened her disheveled dress.

The fabric may have been torn, but her spirit wasn't.

She had a secret to protect, a future to reclaim, a hidden strength she hadn't fully realized.

As the first rays of dawn painted the sky in hues of pink and gold, Louisa stood up, her gaze unwavering.

She would find a way.

Suddenly, a firm hand clamped onto her shoulder. Louisa flinched, whirling around to face her pursuer. Her breath hitched in her throat. It was the woman again, the one in William's hallway, her expression a mask of fury.

"There you are," the woman hissed, her voice barely a whisper. "I need to talk to you ... privately."

Louisa hesitated.

What did this woman want? Another interrogation?

But something in the woman's urgent tone, a hint of fear beneath the anger, compelled Louisa to follow her.

They walked in silence for a while, the woman leading Louisa through a maze of roads and hidden pathways. Finally, they reached a secluded clearing, bathed in the soft light of dawn.

"Who are you?" the woman demanded, her voice low and dangerous. "And what are you doing with my son?"

Louisa's blood ran cold.

Son?

This woman was William's mother.

Her carefully constructed story lay in pieces at her feet.

"I ..." Louisa stammered, her voice cracking under the weight of the woman's gaze. "I ..."

"Don't play coy with me, girl," the woman snapped. "I saw how you were looking at him, the way you tried to ... to ensnare him. You were trying to break him away from his wife-to-be."

"Ensnare him?" Louisa bristled, the anger returning. "I wasn't trying to do any such thing! I ... I care about him."

The woman snorted, a harsh, disbelieving sound. "Care? Don't make me laugh. You're just another nameless female, aren't you? Another pretty face trying to take advantage of his kindness."

Louisa's jaw clenched tight. Before Louisa could unleash a retort fueled by righteous fury, the woman's next words struck her like a physical blow.

"Stay away from him," she commanded, her voice laced with a chilling finality. "He doesn't need your kind of trouble in his life."

Louisa's heart plummeted.

Trouble?

What trouble could she have possibly caused in the brief time she'd known William?

The woman's words, laced with suspicion and disdain, painted a picture of Louisa as a cunning manipulator, a predator preying on William's innocence.

A bitter truth settled in Louisa's stomach.

Even if she revealed herself, even if William believed her story, his mother would never accept her.

The chasm between their social classes as Louisa and not Lady Hastings, the weight of her secret, would forever cast a shadow over their relationship.

Suddenly, the weight of her burden seemed unbearable. What future did she have with William, constantly under suspicion, constantly battling his mother's disapproval? Was this the life she envisioned—a life of secrecy and shadows?

Louisa straightened her back, a newfound resolve hardening her features. Tears welled up in her eyes, but this time they were not tears of self-pity. They were tears of resolve, of a difficult decision made.

"You're right," she said, her voice surprisingly steady. "I won't cause him any more trouble. I'll leave."

The woman seemed surprised by her quick acquiescence, a flicker of something that might have been sympathy crossing her face for a fleeting moment. But it was quickly replaced by hardness.

"Good," she said curtly. "And don't even think about coming back."

Louisa nodded, the lump in her throat making it difficult to speak.

Turning away from the woman, she started walking, her sapphire dress gathering dampness in the morning dew.

Chapter 14: William

William remained rooted to the spot like a statue.

The door to his study hung open still, and the more he stared at it, the more it looked like a silent witness to the scene that had just unfolded before his horrified eyes.

It wasn't just his imagination, right?

Louis... No. It had to have been Louisa. She had stood frozen in the doorway, her soft eyes wide with a hurt that still sliced through him like a physical blow.

She had stood there, looking breathtaking in her sapphire blue dress, but tears had pooled in her eyes.

An overwhelming urge to break free, to cross the room and reach out to her, had warred with the suffocating weight of another hand clinging to his arm.

Lady Jacqueline, her face flushed with the excitement of the tale she had been telling him, had taken one look at Louisa and frowned. And then, very deliberately, she leaned against him, a picture of misplaced intimacy.

He stiffened.

The image they must have presented, him caught in an image with one woman while his eyes fixated on another, was enough to send a wave of nausea crashing over him.

How could he explain this? How could he erase the look of betrayal that flickered across Louisa's face before she vanished like a wisp of smoke?

"William?" Lady Jacqueline's voice, laced with innocent confusion, snapped him out of his thoughts.

He looked down at her, immediately hating the way she touched him. He wanted to snap at her, to tell her to leave him, but he couldn't.

He cleared his throat once, twice. "M-My apologies, Lady Jacqueline," he whispered. "I … I believe I saw someone I knew leaving the house."

The words tasted like ashes in his mouth. But what other explanation could he offer in this suffocating situation? How could he disentangle himself from the viper?

Lady Jacqueline, thankfully, seemed to accept his flimsy excuse. "Oh? It could be nothing." She grinned in a way she probably thought was beautiful, leaning even closer. "Perhaps we should resume our conversation?" she suggested, her voice regaining its practiced poise.

But the suggestion fell on deaf ears. William's mind was a whirlwind of chaotic thoughts, each one more agonizing than the last.

The hurt he saw in Louisa's eyes echoed in his own soul. Had he destroyed any fragile trust that might have existed between them?

Was there any trust between them when her very existence to him for the short time he knew her was a lie?

He couldn't just let this stand.

A solution, desperate and potentially reckless, began to form in his mind.

He had to find her. Now.

"Lady Jacqueline," he began, his voice gaining a steely resolve, "I fear I must cut this visit short. An urgent matter has suddenly arisen that requires my immediate attention."

The surprise on her face was genuine. "But, my lord," she began, disappointment crossing her features.

"I offer my sincerest apologies," he interrupted, his voice firm. He took some steps back, causing her to let go of his arm. "I will arrange for a visit at your earliest convenience to properly explain ..."

He trailed off, unable to bring himself to utter a lie about a non-existent urgent matter. Lady Jacqueline, however, acted like she understood, her disappointment morphing into a thin smile.

"Of course," she said, her voice sweet—a bit too sweet. It grated on his nerves. "Perhaps a walk in the park tomorrow afternoon? We could continue our ... conversation."

William forced a smile. "An excellent suggestion, Lady Jacqueline. Until then."

As she took her leave, a flurry of farewells and polite curtsies, William felt an almost unbearable pressure building within him. He needed to find Louisa, to explain, to apologize ... to understand, to ask questions.

The moment the front door closed behind Lady Jacqueline, William rushed out of the study, his footsteps echoing in the otherwise silent mansion.

He checked every room, his heart pounding a frantic rhythm against his ribs, but Louisa was nowhere to be found.

He stood in the deserted hallway, the silence pressing down on him like a physical weight. Where could she have gone?

Did she leave the estate entirely?

The vastness of the city seemed daunting, an ocean of possibilities with no clue to guide him.

But he had to find her. He raced towards the back of the house, his steps lighter with newfound purpose.

As he arrived outside, a shadowy figure caught his eye.

A woman shrouded in a cloak, her silhouette familiar.

His heart lurched in his throat.

Was it?

"Louisa?" he called out, his voice hoarse with urgency.

The figure remained motionless, a silent silhouette against the luminous night sky.

"Louisa?" he called out again, his voice tinged with a desperation that echoed.

But the name died on his lips as the figure turned, the cloak falling away to reveal a face dark with disappointment—his mother.

What was she doing here?

"William." Her voice, laced with icy disapproval, cut through the night air. "What on earth are you doing out here, calling another woman's name when you should be with your fiancée?"

Shame washed over him, a bitter tide. He couldn't explain.

How could he tell her about Louisa, about the revelation that had shaken his world?

That she was a woman? And that somehow, he had fallen utterly and truly in love with a woman who had a million secrets?

How could he admit to the growing attraction he felt for this woman who lived a life so different from his own?

"Mother, I ... I thought I saw someone I knew," he stammered, his voice constricted.

Her gaze narrowed, her sharp eyes scanning his face with practiced scrutiny. "And who might this woman be, William? Someone more interesting than Lady Jacqueline who is your wife-to-be, I presume?"

The very mention of Lady Jacqueline sent a fresh wave of irritation through him. "Lady Jacqueline has taken her leave," he said curtly. "There was an urgent matter that required my attention."

His mother scoffed, a dismissive sound that spoke volumes. "Don't pretend with me, William. I know about your reluctance to court Lady Jacqueline. But you have given your word, and this family does not go back on their promises."

He knew.

Oh, he knew.

Still, her words were a bitter pill to swallow. He had agreed to court Lady Jacqueline to appease his mother, to fulfill societal expectations.

His heart had remained stubbornly lodged in a place he couldn't find, but now he finally understood.

"Mother," he began, his voice tight with frustration, "I appreciate your concern, but I—"

"No buts, son!" she interrupted, her voice gaining a sharp edge. "You have a duty to this family, to secure its future. Lady Jacqueline is a perfect match—intelligent, well-bred, from a distinguished family. She's everything you need in a wife."

He clenched his fists, the injustice of it all burning in his chest. "But what if I don't want a perfect match, Mother? What if I ..."

He trailed off, the words getting caught in his throat.

"You will do your duty," his mother finished for him, her voice brooking no argument. "That is all that matters."

His shoulders slumped in defeat. There was no reasoning with her. He, the man of the house, felt like a child once again, powerless against her iron will.

"If you'll excuse me, Mother," he said, his voice flat with resignation, "I have a lot on my mind."

He turned away, the cold night air offering a small comfort. As he walked away, a sense of utter despair washed over him.

He had hoped to find Louisa, to bridge the chasm that had opened between them. Now, he was faced with another obstacle—his mother's relentless pursuit of a future he didn't desire.

Arriving at his chambers, he slammed the door shut, the sound echoing like a gunshot through the quiet house.

He sank into a chair, the weight of the world pressing down on him.

He had lost sight of Louisa, his one chance for a connection that transcended social status.

He was trapped in a web of his own making, bound by duty and societal expectations.

The loneliness gnawed at him, a familiar ache that threatened to consume him whole. He had a yearning for a life filled with more than propriety and polite conversation. He craved something real, something genuine, and right now, it felt hopelessly out of reach.

His bitter reality stared him in the face. He had already sealed his fate by agreeing to court Lady Jacqueline.

Denial, a tempting escape route, slammed shut with a resounding thud.

He couldn't deny the truth any longer. Louisa, with her fiery spirit and captivating eyes, had ignited a spark within him he couldn't extinguish.

Guilt gnawed at him, a relentless parasite feeding on his regret.

But despair, however suffocating, wasn't his nature. He wouldn't simply surrender. He wouldn't let things end like this.

A new resolve hardened within him. He would investigate. He would delve into the enigma that was Louisa and uncover the reason for her charade.

He knew she was Lady Hastings.

He remembered the face in the posters.

He remembered every detail of it, and that was why Louis always looked familiar. The female version of that young lad was the woman he had danced with.

He still remembered it.

The same emerald eyes, the same mischievous tilt to her lips ... it was her. Without a doubt, Louis, the enigmatic young man he'd taken under his wing, was Lady Louisa Hastings, a woman of noble birth forced to live a life shrouded in deception.

The woman he had unknowingly fallen for.

Understanding flooded through him, cold and sharp. The fear that flickered in her eyes whenever Lord Thorne's name was mentioned, the constant vigilance, the need for a hidden escape route ... it all made sense now.

Of course, she was hiding.

But why? Hiding from what? What could have driven a woman of her breeding to such drastic measures?

Chapter 15: Louisa

The past few weeks had been a whirlwind of activity at the bookshop. Mr. Abernathy, in his zealous pursuit of finding Louisa a suitable husband, had transformed the quaint shop into a social hub and, working with Esme, provided her with much-needed dresses.

Bless his good heart, but it really doesn't seem to be working, Louisa thought in her mind as she watched the man grab a book from behind the counter.

Every afternoon, a parade of well-dressed gentlemen, each seemingly wealthier and more distinguished than the last, would descend upon Havenwood.

Mr. Abernathy, with a mischievous twinkle in his eye, would introduce them to Louisa, eagerly anticipating the spark of love that he hoped would ignite.

Louisa, however, remained unfazed. The men, while polite and pleasant, were all cut from the same cloth—predictable, conventional, and utterly devoid of the spark she craved.

The spark she so easily had for William.

Later that afternoon, as she was meticulously dusting the shelves, Mr. Abernathy approached her, a conspiratorial grin plastered on his face.

"My dear Louisa," he began, his voice hushed, "I expect a rather distinguished visitor this afternoon. Unfortunately, I have a pressing engagement that I cannot avoid. However, I wouldn't dream of leaving him alone."

Louisa raised an eyebrow, already anticipating his next move. "And what exactly do you propose, Mr. Abernathy?"

"Why, you shall attend to him, of course!" he declared, as if the answer was self-evident. "He's a man of considerable means and influence, and I have a feeling the two of you will hit it off famously. So, would you be so kind as to receive him in my stead?"

"Another one of your schemes, Mr. Abernathy?"

The old man chuckled, his eyes twinkling. "Perhaps. But who knows, this one might be the charm."

Louisa sighed inwardly.

Mr. Abernathy's matchmaking schemes were becoming increasingly transparent.

She knew this "distinguished visitor" was just another attempt to secure her future through a convenient marriage.

"Very well," she said, her voice laced with a hint of resignation, "but if he bores me to tears, I shall hold you personally responsible."

Mr. Abernathy was unfazed by her playful threat. "I have the utmost faith in your charm, Louisa. Now, go change into your dress. You can't find a man to marry dressed like a man!"

Louisa smiled and nodded, glancing down at the men's clothes she still wore in disguise. Mr. Abernathy had told her to stop wearing them since he now knew, but Louisa couldn't bring herself to it. She knew William often frequented the bookshop, and she couldn't afford him knowing she was a woman, not when he already had someone by his side.

With a sigh, she retreated to her room and quickly changed into a simple yet elegant gown.

The fabric, a soft shade of lavender, accentuated her eyes and brought a touch of femininity to her appearance.

She prepared herself for another afternoon of polite conversation and forced smiles.

The visitor arrived shortly after Mr. Abernathy's departure. He was a tall, imposing man with a neatly trimmed beard and a stern expression. He introduced himself as Lord Dimitri, and Louisa immediately sensed an air of arrogance about him.

The conversation, as she had anticipated, was stilted and predictable. Lord Dimitri spoke of his vast estates and influential connections, while Louisa offered polite but noncommittal responses.

As the minutes dragged on, Louisa found herself growing increasingly bored. She yearned for a conversation that went beyond societal expectations and superficial pleasantries.

Finally, unable to bear the monotony any longer, she decided to take a different approach.

"Lord Dimitri," she began, her voice taking on a playful lilt, "tell me, what is the most daring thing you've ever done?"

Lord Dimitri blinked, taken aback by her unexpected question. "Daring?" he repeated, a frown creasing his brow. "Well, I suppose I once ..."

He launched into a tedious tale of a successful business venture, completely missing the point of Louisa's question.

Louisa stifled a sigh. This was exactly what she had expected.

"No, no," she interrupted gently. "I mean something truly daring. Something that pushed you outside your comfort zone, something that made you feel truly alive."

Lord Dimitri looked flustered. He stammered for a moment, then shook his head. "I cannot say that I have done anything of that nature. A gentleman of my standing must always conduct himself with propriety."

Louisa's lips twitched into a wry smile. "Propriety," she mused. "Such a dull and limiting concept. I suppose a life lived entirely within the confines of societal expectations must be quite ... uneventful."

To her surprise, Lord Dimitri burst out laughing.

The sound was rich and genuine, a stark contrast to the stiff and formal demeanor he had displayed earlier.

"You're right, Miss Hastings," he admitted, a twinkle in his eyes. "Perhaps I have been a bit too rigid in my adherence to propriety. Life is meant to be lived, not merely observed."

Louisa found herself drawn to his sudden change of character. This was the man she had glimpsed beneath the facade, a man with a sense of humor and a willingness to challenge societal norms.

They continued their conversation, delving into topics that were far more engaging than the usual polite chatter. They discussed literature, philosophy, and even the latest political developments, each challenging the other's perspectives in a stimulating way.

As the afternoon wore on, Louisa realized that she was genuinely enjoying Lord Dimitri's company. He was intelligent, witty, and he possessed a refreshing openness that she found quite appealing.

However, despite the pleasant exchange and the undeniable spark of intellectual connection, Louisa couldn't help but feel a sense of something missing. There was a certain emotional depth, a romantic spark, that was absent from their interaction.

When it was time for Lord Dimitri to leave, he surprised her once again. He took her hand in his and gently kissed the back of her palm.

"It has been a pleasure conversing with you, Miss Hastings," he said, his voice warm and sincere. "Please give my regards to Mr. Abernathy."

Louisa watched him leave, a smile lingering on her lips. He had been a breath of fresh air, a welcome change from the predictable gentlemen she had encountered before.

As the door to the bookshop closed, Louisa turned and froze. Her heart hammered against her ribs as she saw William standing in the doorway, his eyes fixed on her.

Instinct took over, and she turned to flee. She couldn't let him see her like this, not when he was already engaged to Lady Jacqueline.

"Louisa," he called out, his voice a mixture of surprise and concern.

She paused with her back to him, her mind racing. He wasn't supposed to know. He wasn't supposed to see her like this.

"There's no need to hide," William said gently, taking a step closer. "I know who you are."

Louisa's breath hitched in her throat. Her carefully constructed disguise, her meticulously guarded secret, was shattered in an instant.

She slowly turned around, her heart pounding like a drum in her chest. William's face was unreadable, a mix of emotions swirling in his eyes.

"You ... you know?" she stammered, her voice barely above a whisper.

William nodded, his gaze unwavering. "I saw you at the river. I recognized you immediately."

Louisa's mind raced. *So, what I heard that day at the river was him? He saw me? He has known all this while?*

Questions ran through her mind as waves of emotions washed over her—relief, fear, a flicker of hope. She had been living in constant fear of discovery, and now it had finally happened.

William took a step closer, his eyes searching hers. "Louisa, why didn't you tell me? Why did you lie to me?"

His voice betrayed a mix of hurt and confusion, and Louisa felt a pang of guilt. She had deceived him. She had built a wall of lies between them.

"I ... I had to," she whispered, her voice barely audible. "It was the only way to protect myself."

"Protect yourself from what?" William pressed, his voice hardening. "What are you hiding, Louisa?"

He stalked closer, one question at a time, his gaze pinning her to the spot. Louisa felt cornered, trapped by the weight of his questions and the intensity of his presence.

His scent, a mix of leather and wood smoke, filled her senses, causing a stir inside her. It was a familiar scent, one that had become inextricably linked to him in her mind. It comforted and aroused her, a dangerous combination in the face of the impossible situation they found themselves in.

Her back hit the wall, her heart pounding against her ribs. They were both aware of the unspoken truth—the spark between them, the undeniable pull they felt towards each other.

But there was nothing to be done.

William was already engaged to Lady Jacqueline, and she had another lord who seemed genuinely interested in her. She couldn't afford to waste time, not when her life was in danger.

Taking a deep breath, she straightened her back and met his gaze with a defiant glint in her eyes.

"I owe you no explanation, William," she said, her voice firm despite the tremor in her heart.

She turned to leave, desperate to escape the suffocating tension and the weight of his questions.

But William reached out and gently grasped her arm, stopping her in her tracks.

"Wait," he said, his voice low and urgent. "Lord Dimitri. What was he doing here?"

Louisa hesitated, her mind racing. She couldn't reveal her true intentions. Not yet.

"Lord Dimitri," she said, her voice carefully neutral. "He is a suitor."

William's jaw clenched tight, his eyes narrowing. "A suitor?"

"Yes, a suitor," she admitted. "I cannot afford to remain unmarried any longer. Time is not on my side, not when my life is in danger."

William's eyes widened in surprise. "Your life is in danger? What do you mean?"

Louisa looked away, unable to meet his gaze. She couldn't tell him anything.

She didn't want to pull him into her mess. Worse still, his mother had told her to stay away from him, and that's what she was going to do.

"It's a long story," she said evasively, her voice firm. "One you don't have the right to know."

With that, she turned and walked away, leaving William standing there, his face etched with a mixture of emotions.

Chapter 16: William

The carriage rattled along the cobblestone streets, each bump a jarring echo of the turmoil William felt within.

Days had bled into each other, a monotonous blur punctuated by stolen glances and a gnawing sense of helplessness.

Louisa had basically become a ghost in his life.

Every attempt to initiate a conversation ended in a polite or sometimes harsh dismissal, her emerald eyes clouded with an apprehension he couldn't decipher.

She was avoiding him.

That much was clear.

Then there was the weight of societal expectations that sat heavy on his chest.

Lady Jacqueline, who tried too hard to be sweet and kind in her own right, was a constant reminder of the path he had seemingly chosen.

He should be content.

The woman was beautiful and looked like she wanted nothing more than to be his wife.

Yet, the thought of another man—Lord Dimitri, with his calm demeanor and gentle gaze—claiming Louisa's hand in marriage sent a surge of primal possessiveness coursing through him.

It was a sentiment unfitting for a gentleman in his position, a primal urge to respond with violence—something entirely inappropriate in polite society.

"William," Lady Jacqueline's voice, with a hint of playful curiosity, broke through his dark reverie. "Isn't that your bookstore?"

The familiar exterior of the bookstore loomed ahead, its golden lettering a cruel reminder of happier times. His heart hammered a frantic rhythm against his ribs.

"Indeed, it is," he managed, his voice a touch hoarse.

Louisa was in there.

But she didn't want to see him.

He wondered why she ran from him so much.

He could help her.

He could ...

"Perhaps we could stop for a moment?" she suggested, a hint of a smile gracing her lips. "It would be delightful to see the things that inspire my future husband."

There was an undercurrent to her words, a shrill possessiveness that made the hair on his skin stand straight. It wasn't just the bookstore itself she was interested in; it was the world he inhabited, a world that, until recently, included Louisa.

The thought of Lady Jacqueline, with her genteel manners and innocent demeanor, interacting with Louisa under the guise of wifely curiosity was unbearable.

But he had no choice. Denying her request would be seen as churlish, a display of possessiveness over something that would only raise suspicion.

"Of course," he gritted out, forcing a smile that felt brittle and unconvincing even to himself. "I would be happy to show you around."

The carriage lurched to a halt. William stepped out, casting a glance towards the door.

There was no sign of Louisa. No wisp of her soft wavy hair framed in the window.

Was she inside?

He hoped not.

Lady Jacqueline took his arm, a gesture heavy with unspoken claims, and they entered the bookstore.

The bell above the shop door chimed as they entered, the familiar scent of old paper and leather enveloping him. He hoped he had not made a mistake.

He hoped Louisa would not be there.

His gaze swept over the empty shop floor, and he almost smiled in relief. Then, a figure emerged from behind a towering stack of leather-bound volumes.

A woman. It was clearly a woman.

His breath hitched in his throat. It was Louisa, her fiery wavy hair cascading down her back, her emerald eyes wide with surprise.

It seemed she had let go of her charade as a man.

For a fleeting moment, a spark of recognition flared in her eyes, then, just as quickly, it was extinguished.

She walked behind the counter. "Good day, Lord William. How may I help you today?"

And then she froze, her body rigid with tension as Lady Jacqueline approached her with a practiced smile.

"Well, hello there!" Lady Jacqueline chirped, her voice brimming with a false warmth that grated on William's nerves. "William never mentioned having such a lovely young lady working here. What is your name, dear?"

Louisa remained silent, her gaze flitting between them.

"Does she not speak?" she asked William in that small, innocent lying voice.

"She does." It was Louisa that spoke. "Her name is Louisa."

"Louisa? That sounds familiar, doesn't it, William?" Lady Jacqueline prompted, turning towards him. "I thought your clerk was a young man."

Before he could answer, she continued, a malicious glint in her eyes, "Oh. Perhaps you ... fired the young fellow? Those rumors about being so close and friendly with such an unsuitable employee must have been quite the bother. Clever of you to hire a female with the same name to avoid suspicion."

She let out a tinkling laugh that lacked any genuine mirth. "You must have been very ... fond of that young lad," she added, the sweetness dripping from her lips like poison, "if you hired the female version of him."

William's jaw clenched tight. He wanted to refute her vile insinuations, to expose the ugliness of her veiled accusations, but Louisa beat him to it.

"Lady Jacqueline," she said, her voice surprisingly steady, "there has been no firing. I have always been the clerk here, under Lord William's employ."

Her words, delivered with quiet dignity, shattered the air of veiled hostility. Lady Jacqueline blinked, momentarily surprised by the unexpected response.

"But, my dear," Lady Jacqueline purred, her smile turning strained, "a woman working in such a ... public establishment? It simply isn't done. Not only is it inappropriate, but it could cause a great deal of scandal for my fiancé."

The insinuation hung heavy in the air. She was trying to belittle Louisa, to paint her as desperate and unconventional, a woman who defied societal norms.

But Louisa met her gaze with an unwavering defiance. "A woman," she countered, her voice laced with quiet strength, "is perfectly capable of conducting herself with propriety in any environment. And as for a fiancé," she continued, a hint of amusement flickering in her eyes, "I believe that is a matter yet to be decided. You're not married yet. So don't be so worried, my lady."

The barb landed with pinpoint accuracy. Lady Jacqueline's smile faltered completely, replaced by a mask of barely concealed anger. She had clearly not anticipated such a poised and intelligent response.

The atmosphere in the bookstore crackled with unspoken tension. Louisa stood firm, her chin held high, a beacon of defiance against Lady Jacqueline's petty barbs. William felt a surge of admiration for her, for her unwavering spirit and her refusal to be cowed by societal pressures.

Lady Jacqueline, however, was not finished. Her lips pursed into a thin line, but William was done. He took her arm.

"Now that you've seen my bookstore, we shall leave now," he said and promptly dragged her out.

Was this the woman he planned to marry?

***

Later that night, William, arm linked with Lady Jacqueline, felt a suffocating sense of unreality as he walked into a glittering ballroom that buzzed with a cacophony of music and polite chatter. The silk of her glove felt stiff against his palm, a stark contrast to the memory of Louisa's fiery spirit that was etched in his mind.

He wanted to be anywhere else, but Lady Jacqueline had accepted the invitation on his behalf. He had even tried staying behind, but he had quickly grown tired of arguing with his mother, so there he was, keeping up appearances.

He looked at Lady Jacqueline. In her customary pale blue, he had to admit that she was a picture of elegance. Her blonde hair shimmered under the crystal chandeliers, and her smile, practiced and polite, never quite reached her eyes. She was everything a proper society lady should be—graceful, charming, and utterly predictable.

But it was Louisa who consumed his thoughts. The memory of her defiance in the bookstore, the glint of emerald fire in her eyes, lingered like a phantom sensation.

He scanned the faces in the crowd, a desperate yearning twisting his gut.

Then, a vision materialized at the edge of the ballroom. Louisa. Her auburn hair, usually a fiery cascade, was now tamed into an intricate chignon, adorned with a single pearl comb that shimmered in the light. Her gown, a vibrant emerald green that mirrored her eyes, hugged her curves in a way that was both elegant and undeniably alluring.

Diamonds sparkled around her neck and adorned her ears, their brilliance somehow muted by the natural luminescence radiating from her. But it was the way she carried herself, a regal grace that belied her assumed station as a clerk, that truly captured his breath.

Beside her stood Lord Dimitri, a figure William was starting to loathe with growing intensity. The man's happy smirk and stable gaze as he leaned towards Louisa in conversation sent a jolt of jealousy coursing through him.

They made an undeniably striking couple. His imposing stature complemented her delicate beauty, and a faint blush dusted her cheeks as she listened to him speak.

William hated it.

Chapter 17: Louisa

Crystal chandeliers cast a warm glow on the elegantly dressed couples swirling across the dance floor.

Louisa stood beside Lord Dimitri, his latest attempt at a witty remark failing to bring more than a polite smile.

Her gaze was drawn across the room, where William stood with Lady Jacqueline. They were engaged in conversation, their bodies close, their laughter echoing in the air.

A pang of jealousy, sharp and unexpected, pierced Louisa's heart. She had convinced herself that she was moving on, that she had accepted the harsh reality of her situation. But seeing him with Lady Jacqueline, the woman he was supposed to marry, brought back the raw ache of what could have been.

"Are you alright, Miss Hastings?" Lord Dimitri asked, his voice laced with concern.

Louisa quickly schooled her features into a neutral expression. "I'm well. Thank you," she said, forcing a smile.

Music began to play, a lively waltz that filled the room with infectious rhythm. Lord Dimitri extended his hand, his eyes twinkling with anticipation.

"May I have this dance?" he asked.

Louisa hesitated for a moment, then placed her hand in his. He led her onto the dance floor, their movements graceful and synchronized.

As they danced, Louisa couldn't help but steal glances at William, who was dancing with Lady Jacqueline.

Their movements were perfectly synchronized, a routine that spoke of familiarity and intimacy.

She tried to focus on her conversation with Lord Dimitri, his witty remarks and engaging stories, but her mind kept drifting back to William, to the stolen moments they had shared, to the connection that felt so real and yet so forbidden.

She forced herself to focus on what Lord Dimitri was saying.

"I must say, Miss Hastings," Lord Dimitri remarked, a playful glint in his eyes, "you have a most captivating wit. Your repartee is quite impressive."

Louisa offered him a polite smile. "Thank you, Lord Dimitri. I try my best."

"Well, your best is certainly commendable," he continued, his voice low and alluring. "I find myself quite ... captivated."

She felt a blush creeping up her neck, but she quickly masked it with a light laugh. "Oh, Lord Dimitri, you flatter me."

As they continued their conversation, Louisa tried her best to keep her mind from wandering.

She focused on the dance, patterns of the ballroom floor, the vibrant colors of the decorations ... anything to distract herself from the magnetic pull she felt towards William across the room.

But fate, it seemed, had a cruel sense of humor.

When the music reached the part where partners were to be changed, Louisa found herself facing William.

The moment their eyes met, the tension in the air crackled. It was a silent conversation, a dance of unspoken emotions conveyed through fleeting glances and the lingering touch of their hands as they exchanged partners.

For a brief, exhilarating moment, Louisa was back in his arms. The familiar warmth of his body, the intoxicating scent of his cologne ... it all sent a jolt of electricity through her.

"Miss Hastings," William said, his voice a low rumble that sent a jolt down her spine. "It's a pleasure to see you again."

"The pleasure is mine, Lord Blackwood," Louisa replied, her voice steady despite the turmoil within her.

As they began to dance, the world around them faded away. Their bodies moved in perfect harmony, their steps echoing the rhythm of their unspoken desires.

"You look ... radiant tonight," William murmured, his eyes tracing the lines of her face.

"And you, Lord Blackwood," Louisa said, her voice barely a whisper.

The air between them was thick with unspoken longing, a bittersweet reminder of what could have been. They danced in silence, their bodies speaking a language only they understood.

But the moment was fleeting. All too soon, the music changed again, and she was back in Lord Dimitri's arms.

The contrast was stark. The joy and excitement she had felt with William was replaced by a dull ache of disappointment.

As the dance ended, Louisa forced a smile and thanked Lord Dimitri for the dance.

"A delightful dance, Miss Hastings," Lord Dimitri said, his voice polite but lacking the spark that had been present before.

Louisa forced a smile. "Indeed, Lord Dimitri. Thank you."

She knew she had to move on, to focus on her own future, but the memory of that brief, stolen moment with William lingered.

Needing some air, Louisa excused herself and slipped out into the garden. The cool night air washed over her, offering a brief respite from the stifling atmosphere of the ballroom.

As she walked, gazing at the moonlit sky, a sudden movement caught her eye. Her aunt, Lady Beatrice, stood at the edge of the garden, her face contorted in a mask of feigned relief.

"Louisa!" she cried out, her voice laced with desperation. "Please, you have to come back home."

Louisa's heart pounded in her chest. She had known this moment would come and had dreaded it for weeks, but seeing her aunt standing before her sent a wave of panic through her.

"I won't go with you!" she cried out, her voice trembling with defiance. "I'm not going back to that life!"

Lady Beatrice's face crumpled, and she reached out a hand, her eyes filled with what seemed like genuine concern. "Louisa darling, please, listen to me. You're in danger here. We need to get you back home, where you're safe."

Louisa was taken aback.

This was not the cold, calculating aunt she knew.

This woman seemed genuinely worried, her voice pleading, her eyes filled with an almost convincing desperation.

"What are you talking about?" Louisa asked, her voice wary. "Why would I be in danger here?"

Lady Beatrice hesitated, then leaned in closer, her voice dropping to a conspiratorial whisper. "There are people after you, Louisa. Powerful people who mean you harm. You must come with me now."

Louisa's mind raced. This was absurd. Who would be after her? And why would her aunt, the person who wanted to hurt her, suddenly be so concerned?

"Aunt Beatrice, this doesn't make any sense," she said, her voice firm despite the rising fear in her chest. "You've never been this ... emotional. What's going on?"

Lady Beatrice's eyes darted around nervously. "There's no time to explain, Louisa. We must leave. Now!"

She reached out and grabbed Louisa's arm, her grip surprisingly strong.

Something was wrong. Louisa sensed it immediately and tried to pull away, but her aunt held on tight.

"Let go of me!" Louisa cried, her voice rising in panic.

Aunt Beatrice's face hardened. "You don't have a choice, Louisa," she hissed, her voice low and menacing.

Suddenly, her hands shot up, and two burly men emerged from the shadows.

Louisa's breath hitched in her throat. This was it. They were here to take her back.

She backed away, her eyes darting around for an escape route. But there was nowhere to go. She was trapped.

The men advanced, their faces devoid of any emotion. Louisa knew she couldn't fight them. They were too strong, too determined.

Suddenly, one of the men lunged forward and grabbed Louisa's arm. She cried out in surprise and tried to pull away, but his grip was strong.

In the struggle, she stumbled and fell, scraping her knee and palm on the rough gravel path. She hissed in pain, tears welling up in her eyes.

But just as the man was about to grab her again, a voice boomed from behind.

"Leave her alone!"

Louisa turned to see William standing there, his face full of fury.

The men hesitated, surprised by the unexpected intervention. William, however, was undeterred. He strode forward, his stance defiant, his eyes blazing with anger.

"This is none of your concern, Lord Blackwood," Aunt Beatrice said, her voice laced with venom.

"On the contrary, it is," William countered, his voice firm and unwavering. "Miss Hastings is under my protection."

The men exchanged glances, unsure of how to proceed. Aunt Beatrice, however, was not about to back down.

"She's my niece," she insisted, her voice shrill with desperation. "I have every right to take her home."

"Not if she doesn't want to go," William retorted, his voice laced with steel.

The tension in the air was thick, the scene hanging in a precarious balance.

As the men hesitated, William took the opportunity to move closer to Louisa. He placed a protective hand on her shoulder, his touch sending a jolt of electricity through her.

"Don't worry, Louisa," he said, his voice low and reassuring. "I won't let them take you."

He looked back at Aunt Beatrice and her goons and then said, "I'm certain I do not need to tell you this, but I will. If I see you touch anything of mine, or harm anyone that belongs to me, Lady Beatrice, you know exactly what the punishment will be."

He turned to Louisa, his face softening as he looked at her.

"Are you alright?" he asked, his voice filled with concern.

Louisa nodded, her voice trembling. "Yes, I think so. Just a scrape."

He knelt beside her, gently taking her hand in his. "Come with me."

He helped her up, his touch sending a comforting warmth through her.

As they stood together, the danger momentarily averted, Louisa knew that she wasn't alone. William was there for her, and for the first time, she felt hope amidst the chaos and uncertainty.

Chapter 18: William

Cold fury burned in William's veins, fueled by the heady cocktail of everything that had just happened.

He had seen Louisa leaving the ball, her supposed fiancé nowhere in sight, but after some minutes she had not returned. Since her suitor would not go looking for her, he decided to do it himself.

He had walked out of the heated ballroom, thinking to find her taking some fresh air, but instead, he had seen two burly men surrounding her, their faces tight with malice.

Beside them stood an older woman he remembered. Her aunt.

The scene unfolded in a blur. It was obvious what was happening.

They had come to take her away, and she obviously didn't want to leave with them.

He didn't stop to think. He just took action and intervened, putting a stop to everything.

As they realized who he was, their bravado was quickly replaced by fear, and they scurried away into the night, leaving Louisa trembling in the wake of their aggression.

He took her hand and helped her up, the warmth of her skin a stark contrast to the chilling encounter moments ago.

"Come with me," he said, his voice gruff with unspoken emotions.

She looked at him, her emerald eyes wide with shock and a touch of gratitude.

A carriage clattered to a halt in front of them, summoned with a frantic wave of his hand. "Mr. Abernathy's residence," he barked at the driver, the words leaving his lips with a curtness he didn't recognize.

"I ... Lord William, I don't think we should leave the ball like this," Louisa said. "People ... Lord Dimitri—"

"Who has not so much as blinked since you left the ball, not caring for where you could be? Get in the carriage, Lady Hastings," he growled angrily.

She glared at him but didn't protest.

Taking her elbow, he gently helped her into the carriage. She settled onto the plush velvet seat, her hand still clasped tightly in his. The silence stretched between them, thick with unspoken tension.

Then she asked, "Why are we going to Mr. Abernathy's residence?"

He cleared his throat. "Mr. Abernathy's is a safe haven," he said, his voice resolute.

Mr. Abernathy was the only person he could trust with Louisa's secret and protection apart from himself.

Taking her to his own home was unthinkable. A scandal of epic proportions would erupt. Leaving her at the bookstore, especially after the encounter with the thugs, was simply not an option.

Mr. Abernathy's home, a sanctuary tucked away on a quiet cobblestone street, seemed like the only reasonable solution, at least for now.

As the carriage rattled towards its destination, the weight of the situation settled upon William. Louisa, with her fiery spirit and captivating beauty, had somehow become entangled in a web of secrets and dangers. And he, bound by his feelings, swore to protect her.

The journey to Mr. Abernathy's felt less like a carriage ride and more like a descent into a future both exhilarating and terrifying. He couldn't ignore her plight, nor the undeniable connection that simmered between them. His head spun with a thousand questions, but one thing remained clear: he wouldn't abandon Louisa. Not now, not ever.

***

The carriage lurched to a halt before Mr. Abernathy's quaint brick townhouse. Relief washed over William as the kindly bookseller emerged, his brow furrowed with concern upon seeing their grim expressions.

Quickly, William explained the situation.

Mr. Abernathy ushered them inside, his concern deepening as he took in Louisa's pale face and trembling hands.

With a gentle smile, he offered her a spare room for the night and brought a basin, a washcloth, and a soothing balm.

"For your wounds, my dear," he said, and bid them good night.

Louisa turned to William and inclined her head. "Thank you for helping me today, my lord. Good night."

But before she could retreat into the room, William found himself walking toward her.

She stopped, eyes wide. "Lord William?"

"Let me in."

Her eyes widened even more. "Pardon? This is my chamber."

"I can see that."

"Then I most definitely can't allow you—"

"I just want to help you clean your wounds, Lady Hastings," he cut in. "You obviously can't do it alone."

"I ... I could try."

"You're truly a stubborn woman. Do you know that?"

"So I've been told all my life. If mending my wounds won't work, I believe sleep would be the best remedy, Lord William," she said, her voice betraying a weariness that tugged at his heart.

A wry smile touched William's lips. "Sleep can wait," he countered, his voice husky. "There are ... matters that require immediate attention. We can go into the drawing room."

She sighed and allowed him to lead her to the drawing room. "You've become quite ungentlemanly these days, Lord William," she teased, her voice a mere whisper.

"Indeed," he replied, the word leaving his lips with a sigh as he stepped closer. "Perhaps a little too concerned for a mere employee's well-being."

She scoffed, but said nothing as William gently guided her into the drawing room. The dim candlelight cast long shadows, heightening the intimacy of the moment.

The banter that had masked their simmering emotions gave way to a charged silence.

The air crackled with unspoken desires, a dangerous current that threatened to break the fragile dam of propriety.

Louisa, her emerald eyes shimmering with a newfound vulnerability, sank into the chair. William's gaze followed her every movement, like a hungry animal.

"Let me see," he commanded, his voice husky and deep, making her gasp softly.

She lifted a hand, revealing a shallow scrape on her palm, the crimson staining the pale flesh in stark contrast to the pristine lace of her evening gown.

A wave of anger surged through him again, but he swallowed it.

Carefully, William knelt before her, the gaslight casting flickering shadows on the wall. His breath hitched as he brushed a stray strand of hair from her face.

With a tenderness that surprised even himself, he examined the scrape.

"It ... it's nothing serious," she murmured, her voice a mere whisper that trailed down his skin.

But it was everything.

In that moment, all thoughts of societal expectations, of duty and propriety, faded away. All that remained was the undeniable pull between them, a yearning so intense it threatened to consume him whole.

And then, with a tremor in his hand, William dipped a damp cloth into the basin and began to tend to her wound.

The simple act of touching her, every brush of his hand against hers, sent a jolt of electricity through him.

Time seemed to slow, the only sound the gentle murmur of his voice and the ragged rhythm of their breaths. As he treated the scrape, his gaze lingered on the delicate curve of her wrist, the pulse fluttering beneath the skin a silent invitation.

The air grew thick with unspoken desire, an intoxicating mixture of concern and yearning that defied definition. The room felt charged, the space between them shrinking with each passing moment.

He finished and stood up, going to throw the water away when she spoke up again.

"There's another," she said, her voice low.

The single word shattered the intoxicating haze enveloping William.

He forced himself back, putting more physical distance between them. "Another wound?" he managed, his voice hoarse.

Louisa, gaze downcast, slowly lifted the hem of her emerald gown, revealing a scraped knee.

William stood there, his body taut with conflicting emotions—concern, desire, and a growing anger.

"Would you …?" she began, her cheeks flushed a delicate pink.

The question hung in the air, unfinished but understood.

Taking a deep breath, William met her gaze. "Of course," he said, his voice a low rumble.

With a measured pace, he approached once more. This time, however, his movements were purposeful, devoid of the earlier hesitancy. As he knelt before her again, the nearness of her sent a jolt through his system.

The delicate lace of her gown brushed against his hand as he lifted it further, exposing the full extent of the scrape.

He didn't breathe.

He couldn't.

With a trembling hand, he dipped the cloth into the basin once more. The water, cool against his skin, offered a fleeting respite from the inferno burning within him.

The room, filled with the soft glow of the candlelight, seemed to shrink, the focus narrowing to the two of them, two souls caught in a dance of forbidden emotions. Each brush of his hand against her skin was an unspoken plea, a question hanging heavy in the air.

Suddenly, Louisa reached out, her hand hovering over his. The touch was light, a mere feather against his skin, yet he felt it keenly. Her eyes, filled with apprehension and yearning, held his captive.

"William," she breathed, her voice barely a whisper.

His name, spoken in such a way, was a siren call, a final push towards the precipice.

"Thank you," she murmured, her voice soft and beautiful. "For everything."

Taking a deep breath, William forced himself to step back. "It is nothing," he replied, his voice gruff, betraying the turmoil within. "Any gentleman would have done the same."

But the lie tasted bitter on his tongue. The truth was, no other gentleman would have found himself so captivated by a mere bookseller's assistant, so willing to breach the boundaries of propriety for her sake.

The silence stretched between them, thick with unspoken emotions.

"William," Louisa finally said, her emerald eyes shimmering with newfound determination, "I need to tell you something."

With a nod, he encouraged her to speak. "Please," he said, his voice low, "tell me everything."

And so, she did. The tale that spilled from her lips was one of betrayal and deceit. She spoke of a tyrannical aunt, a woman who held her future hostage, forcing Louisa to marry lord Thorne, a man she despised.

As she finished her story, a heavy silence descended upon the room.

"I understand now," he said finally, his voice low and measured. "The urgency, the need for a suitor to protect you."

Louisa met his gaze, a flicker of hope igniting in her emerald eyes. "Yes. Apart from Lord Dimitri, there is no one," she admitted, a tremor in her voice betraying her despair. "No one who would ... who could ..."

Before she could finish, he cut her off. "There is someone," he declared, the words tumbling from his lips with a certainty that surprised even him.

Shock flickered across her face, swiftly replaced by a flicker of suspicion. "Who?" she breathed.

"Me," he said, the word a thunderclap in the quiet room. "I would, Louisa."

Louisa's jaw clenched, her eyes widening in disbelief. "William, you can't be serious!" she exclaimed. "This is ... out of the question. You have a fiancée."

"Hear me out, Louisa," he said. "I made no promise to anyone. I will break off our courtship. I don't care what anyone has to say about it." His gaze locked with hers, willing her to see the truth in his eyes. "I will marry you ... protect you. Always. Do you want that?"

The air crackled with unspoken tension as Louisa considered his proposal. The color had drained from her face, leaving her pale and vulnerable.

"Why?" she finally whispered. "Why would you do this for me, William?"

Because he loved her.

"Because you deserve better, Louisa," he said instead, his voice a low rumble. "Because you are a woman of intelligence, of spirit, and you deserve a life free from fear and manipulation. And I wish to help." He met her gaze unflinchingly. "Will you marry me, Louisa?"

Chapter 19: Louisa

The sting of antiseptic on her scraped knee was a pinprick compared to the turmoil churning within Louisa. William's unexpected proposal had thrown her into a whirlwind of emotions, leaving her breathless and bewildered.

His words echoed in her mind, "Will you marry me, Louisa?"

A part of her, the part that had been secretly harboring feelings for him for weeks, soared with joy.

The thought of being his wife, of escaping the clutches of her aunt and the life she desperately wanted to leave behind, was intoxicating.

But another part, a more cautious and cynical voice, whispered warnings.

Why would he offer to marry her, a woman with a tarnished reputation? Was it simply out of pity? A misguided sense of chivalry?

Yet, in that moment, a flicker of hope ignited within her. Marriage to William, even if born out of a sense of duty, offered a chance at escape, a chance to break free from the clutches of her past.

Taking a deep breath, Louisa met his gaze, her voice steady despite the tremor in her heart. "I accept, William. I'll marry you."

William looked up at her with the most beautiful smile she had ever seen in her life. "That's perfect, Lady Hastings."

She couldn't believe it was happening.

She was going to marry William. It sounded like a dream.

As she watched William tend to his own scraped knuckles, the silence in the room felt thick with unspoken emotions.

The air crackled with a tension that was both thrilling and terrifying.

That was when she had a realization that sent a jolt through her, leaving her breathless and trembling.

She was in love with William.

The truth hit her like a bolt of lightning, illuminating the whirlwind of emotions she had been experiencing. The stolen glances, the shared laughter, the way his touch made her feel … it all made sense now.

Without thinking, without considering the consequences, she blurted out the words that had been trapped inside her, "I love you, William."

The words hung in the air, heavy with emotion. She watched his face, waiting for a response, a reflection of the feelings she now knew burned brightly within her.

But his face remained impassive, his expression unreadable. A cold knot of dread formed in her stomach.

"Louisa," he began, his voice low and measured, "I appreciate your honesty. However, I cannot reciprocate your feelings."

His words were a punch to the gut, shattering the fragile hope that had bloomed in her chest. The pain was sharp, unexpected, and it left her speechless.

Why? Why would he offer to marry her if he didn't love her? The question burned on the tip of her tongue, but she swallowed it down. Pride, or perhaps a need for self-preservation, kept her from voicing it.

Instead, she simply nodded. "I understand, William," she said, her voice choked with emotion.

He cleared his throat, his gaze shifting away from hers. "I will begin my courtship tomorrow. You can expect a formal call."

With that, he turned and walked towards the door, leaving Louisa alone in the drawing room, the weight of his rejection settling upon her like a heavy cloak.

As he left, she couldn't help but wonder. Why? Why would he offer her a marriage of convenience, a loveless union, when his heart clearly belonged elsewhere?

The answer remained a mystery, a puzzle she had no desire to unravel at that moment. The pain of his rejection was too raw, too fresh.

She sat there for a long time, the silence of the room amplifying the echo of her broken heart. The future, once filled with hope and possibility, now stretched before her, bleak and uncertain.

Why?

Just why?

Why would he offer marriage if he felt nothing for her?

The question burned in her mind, a painful reminder of the chasm that separated them.

But pride wouldn't allow her to dwell on it. She had made her choice, a desperate gamble for a chance at freedom. Now, she had to face the consequences. She had to navigate the treacherous waters of a courtship built on a foundation of unspoken truths.

As the night wore on, Louisa found herself unable to sleep. Her mind replayed the events of the evening, the tender touch of William's hands as he tended to her wounds, the warmth of his gaze when their eyes met.

She had fallen in love with him, a truth she had finally acknowledged in the quiet of Mr. Abernathy's drawing room. But his rejection had shattered her illusions, leaving her with a bitter taste of unrequited affection.

The next morning, as the first rays of sunlight filtered through the curtains, Louisa forced herself to rise.

The days that followed were a whirlwind of activity. William, true to his word, began his courtship with an official call, his arrival announced by a flurry of footmen and the clatter of carriage wheels.

He presented himself with impeccable manners and a charming smile, his words laced with wit and genuine interest. Louisa, despite the lingering sting of his rejection, played her part with practiced ease.

Their engagement was announced to the ton, and as expected, it sent ripples of curiosity and speculation through the social circles.

Many were surprised, some intrigued, but most whispered their approval. After all, they had witnessed the undeniable chemistry between them, the way their eyes met and held, the subtle touches that spoke volumes despite the constraints of propriety.

The whispers, however, did not bother Louisa. She had made her choice, and she was determined to see it through. William, she knew, was a man of honor, and his offer, however unconventional, was her ticket to freedom.

One afternoon, while browsing the shelves of her beloved bookshop, Louisa was surprised by a visitor. Lady Jacqueline, her former rival, stood before her, her face displaying sadness and resignation.

"Louisa," she began, her voice low, "I came to offer my congratulations and ... to say goodbye."

Louisa raised an eyebrow, surprised by the unexpected announcement. "Goodbye?"

Lady Jacqueline nodded, a wistful smile playing on her lips. "I cannot bear to remain here, knowing you and William are to be wed. It would be ... too painful."

Louisa understood. Anyone in her position would be unable to tolerate unrequited affection.

"I wish you all the happiness in the world, Louisa. Well, for William mostly, but since you are getting wed to him, I wish the same for you," she continued, her voice sincere. "Take good care of him. He deserves someone strong, someone who can match his spirit."

With that, Lady Jacqueline turned and left, her departure as swift and decisive as her arrival.

Louisa watched her go with a pang of sympathy mixed with a sense of relief. Lady Jacqueline's absence, she realized, would clear the path for her and William, allowing them to build their future without the shadow of the past.

Days later, Louisa arrived at the Blackwood Estate invited by William for a tour.

The carriage rumbled to a halt on the gravel driveway of William's imposing estate. Louisa, adorned in a stunning emerald gown that accentuated her curves, stepped out, her heart pounding with a mixture of anticipation and nervousness.

The grand manor loomed before her, its imposing facade whispering tales of generations past. As she approached the entrance, the imposing oak doors swung open, revealing a flurry of activity.

Footmen in crisp livery bowed low, their voices echoing with a respectful, "Welcome home, Lady Hastings."

Louisa, ever the quick wit, countered with a playful smile, "And a good home it is, wouldn't you agree?"

The footmen chuckled, their faces softening at her unexpected charm. It was a stark contrast to the disdain she had faced in her past life. Here, she was not just tolerated but respected and even admired.

William appeared at the top of the grand staircase, his eyes widening in appreciation as they fell upon her. He descended with a grace that belied his athletic build, a slow smile spreading across his face.

"Louisa," he said, his voice a low rumble that made her bite down on her lips, "you look ... breathtaking."

Louisa raised an eyebrow, her own smile widening. "I try, Lord Blackwood. Though I must confess, I'm not accustomed to such a grand welcome."

"Then allow me to rectify that," he said, extending his hand.

As their fingers brushed, a jolt of electricity coursed through Louisa. The air crackled with unspoken desire, the formal setting unable to contain the raw attraction simmering beneath the surface.

William led her through the opulent halls, his hand lingering on hers a touch longer than necessary. The house, the likes of which had once symbolized her entrapment, felt strangely welcoming, its grandeur mirroring the intensity of her emotions.

They reached a secluded library, its walls lined with leather-bound volumes and adorned with plush armchairs. Fire crackled in the hearth, casting a warm glow on the room and creating an intimate atmosphere that fueled the tension already hanging heavy in the air.

William offered her a cup of wine, his eyes never leaving hers. "I thought we could have a bit of privacy so you can feel more comfortable," he said, his voice low and husky.

Louisa took a sip, the warmth of the wine mirroring the heat rising in her cheeks. "I'm very impressed, William. Thank you."

He set down his glass and moved closer, his presence a tangible force in the small space. "Louisa," he began, his voice barely above a whisper, "you have no idea how much I …"

He stopped abruptly, his gaze intense. His hand reached out to brush a stray strand of hair from her face.

The touch made her shiver from inside out, the unspoken words hanging heavy in the air.

Louisa, her heart pounding in her chest, leaned into his touch, her desire matching his.

Her breath hitched in her throat as William's hand brushed against her cheek. The touch was a featherlight caress. Her heart hammered against her ribs.

He leaned closer, his lips hovering just a hair's breadth from hers. The anticipation was agonizing, the unspoken desire hanging thick in the air. Louisa's body thrummed with a primal longing, her lips parting in silent invitation.

But just as their lips were about to meet, William pulled away.

Frustration flared within Louisa, hot and sharp. She gritted her teeth, the disappointment a bitter pill to swallow.

She wouldn't be dismissed. She wouldn't be left wanting. He had ignited a fire within her, and she wouldn't be denied its satisfaction.

In her mind, she pictured his hand returning to her face, his fingers tracing the curve of her jaw, his thumb brushing the corner of her lips. She imagined the heat of his breath against her skin, the press of his lips against hers, the slow, deliberate exploration of their desires.

Louisa closed her eyes, picturing it all with vivid detail, willing it into existence.

And at that moment, she decided to do everything to bring them closer.

Chapter 20: William

Frustration gnawed at William as he stared down at the financial news in his right hand, the fingers on his left hand pinching the bridge of his nose.

Focus, William, he thought. *Pftt, as if it were that easy.*

The meticulously printed columns and graphs of the weekly news blurred before his eyes, their meaning lost in the fog of his thoughts.

He growled and slammed the paper back on his table, leaning back against his chair and drawing deep breaths to calm himself.

He was hot, cold, warm, and everything in between.

And his study, usually a haven of quiet contemplation, wasn't helping matters. It felt suffocating tonight.

He looked down at his fingers drumming slightly, and even the worn leather armchair he rested on seemed to mock his inability to focus.

The mahogany walls, lined with books on trade and economics, offered no solace. Even the utterly expensive gaslight on his desk, casting warm pools of light on the ornately carved globes and nautical charts, seemed to pulse with his agitation.

The truth was, William wasn't interested in cocoa prices or projected shipping routes.

Well, his brain was, but his mind and heart were consumed by a far more captivating topic: Louisa.

The woman had crashed into his life so abruptly that he didn't know when she got right under his skin and slipped over the very high walls he built all those years ago.

Even though he tried not to, the events of the previous evenings replayed in his mind on a relentless loop.

First, at the ball, the vulnerability in her emerald eyes as she shared her secret, the tremor in her voice as she spoke of her desperation ... all of it sent a fresh wave of protectiveness crashing over him.

He hadn't meant to propose, not really, and especially not like that.

The words had tumbled out, a desperate solution to her predicament that offered the benefit of having her closer. Yet, beneath the practical veneer of his offer, a selfish part of him thrilled at the prospect.

Lord Dimitri obviously wasn't interested in protecting the beautiful woman who could have been his future wife. No. The man was more interested in socializing with businessmen and making business trades while his soon-to-be wife was getting harassed by crazy men.

So, the thought of Louisa, safe and cherished within his home, was a balm to the loneliness that had gnawed at him for far too long.

But with all that came guilt, a bitter companion. The memory of Anna rose before him, and his heart sank.

He had been easily able to accept the fact that he felt so much more for Louisa, but that wasn't what had stopped him when she confessed. No. It was Anna.

William hadn't been able to protect her nor their unborn child. What made him think he could do any better this time?

Shame burned in his gut. How could he even contemplate offering himself to another woman when he still carried the weight of that loss? Louisa deserved more than a marriage built on a foundation of guilt and unhealed wounds.

He yearned to reach out to her, to hold her close, to whisper the words that had been building within him. Yet, the specter of his past held him captive, a silent shackle that bound his tongue and paralyzed his actions.

He was afraid.

He was caught in a snare of his own making. The desperate need to protect Louisa had led him to propose, but in doing so, he had made a bargain that felt increasingly unbearable.

A marriage? Was he truly capable of offering her the happiness she deserved? The love she had so inadvertently confessed to desiring?

With a groan, William pushed himself back from his desk, the worn wood groaning under his weight. He needed air. He needed to escape the suffocating confines of his study.

William stepped out onto the veranda, the cool night air biting at his skin and reminding him that he should have worn his coat.

The moon, pale, beautiful, and almost unearthly, offered scant comfort.

He took a deep breath and felt himself calming a little.

His gaze drifted onto the sprawling gardens that stretched out before him.

His jaw ticked.

Here, amidst the meticulously pruned rose bushes and the gently gurgling fountain, a vision of a future with a family, with laughter echoing through the manicured lawns, had once filled his heart with joy.

His chest tightened as he recalled the dreams he'd woven—dreams shattered by the cruel hand of fate. Could he ever allow himself to dream again? Could he bear the risk of building a future, only to have it snatched away once more?

Goosebumps ran up his arms, not from the night air, but from a sudden movement in the distance.

What was that?

He squinted, the play of moonlight momentarily convincing him that he was seeing things. But no, a figure emerged from the shadows, its silhouette unmistakable against the pale luminescence.

Louisa.

His breath hitched in his throat.

She was beautiful, clad in her silvery, silk nightdress. Her hair, grown out again, cascaded down her back. A thick shawl was wrapped around her shoulder as she walked amongst the lively flowers.

What was she doing out in the fields at this ungodly hour? Had she not retired for the night?

Was she okay?

Worry mingled with the tide of emotions that already threatened to drown him.

Since his unorthodox proposal, a storm had swept through his life. Lady Jacqueline, upon hearing the news, had decided to leave for France with the speed of a startled rabbit. His formidable mother, the dowager countess, had initially expressed her disapproval in tones that could curdle milk. However, faced with William's steely resolve and the very real—and potentially scandalous—possibility of him remaining unmarried, along with Louisa's background as Lady Hastings, his mother later grudgingly consented.

He hadn't given her a choice.

He would marry Louisa anyway.

However, the dowager's approval came with a hefty condition. Louisa, she had declared, would not be residing in the "back of an old bookstore." It wasn't "ladylike," according to her outdated sensibilities.

William had found himself extending an invitation for Louisa to stay at the mansion for the next few days before their wedding.

Living under the same roof had been a perilous proposition. Every stolen glance across the breakfast table, every chance encounter in the hallway, was a brush with fire. Louisa, it seemed, was actively chipping away at the walls he'd erected around his heart.

She'd begun dropping hints about new furniture—tasteful pieces that somehow managed to perfectly complement the existing décor.

She'd hummed along absentmindedly while he played the piano, her voice surprisingly sweet.

Just yesterday, she'd caught him staring at a dusty chessboard in the library, a playful glint in her eyes as she challenged him to a game.

These seemingly innocuous actions, these tiny breaches in their carefully constructed distance, were having a devastating effect on him. He could feel his resolve crumbling, his defenses weakening with each passing day.

Before he could decide whether to approach her or allow her to return to the house unseen, Louisa turned. Their eyes met, and he froze.

She smiled and his heart almost melted.

Louisa started towards him, her movements a graceful dance in the silver light. William knew he should retreat and maintain the precarious distance he'd established, but something within him, a force stronger than his remaining resolve, held him rooted to the spot.

He could only wait, heart thundering in his chest, as Louisa crossed the distance towards him.

She moved towards him, her silver gown whispering against the grass, a vision of grace bathed in moonlight. As she neared, William felt a primal urge to reach out, to draw her close and drown himself in the warmth of her presence.

But restraint, a rusted shield, held him back. He couldn't afford to indulge in such desires. Not yet.

"William," she started, but then her eyes fell on the shirt he wore and they softened. "You look so cold out here," she said, her voice soft and laced with a concern that tugged at his heart.

Before he could stop her, her hand reached out, a feather-light touch brushing against his cheek. The warmth of her skin sent a jolt through him, and he flinched before he could think twice.

Goodness. He couldn't think straight with her here.

"Here," she said, her voice barely a whisper. "Let me stay with you for a while. For warmth, of course."

Her words were laced with a playful smile, yet a deeper meaning flickered in her emerald eyes. A silent invitation, a yearning for a closeness he longed to reciprocate.

"Louisa," he began, his voice hoarse, "we should not be doing this."

"Why not?" she countered, her voice laced with a playful challenge. "Are we not soon to be husband and wife? Surely a little closeness is not amiss?"

Her words were a siren call, a temptation he longed to surrender to.

He turned to her, unable to stop the twitch of his lips.

"Of course, it's not," he said carefully, his own hands going up to touch the soft strands of her hair. Before his wary mind could weigh in, he said, "Warmth from you, dear Louisa, is always appreciated."

She smiled, but it seemed she saw past his cheerfulness and into what worried him.

William sniffled. Perhaps he had really caught a cold. "It's late. We should go inside."

He turned away, his heart a leaden weight in his chest.

She caught his wrist.

"William," Louisa's voice came, a tremor running through it. "What's wrong?"

"Nothing," he tried to lie. He didn't want to worry her with his own thoughts. "Just a sudden chill."

She smiled softly. "It doesn't feel like that."

He remained silent.

"You should know that I'm always here for you, William. Here to be with you, to comfort you," she said. "Not just as an engaged couple, but as friends as well."

He didn't know what to say. She stepped closer to him, offering comfort as she could.

This act softened William' heart, but he shook his head. "I do want to tell you, but I don't want to burden you with my feelings."

"Why?"

"I want you to remain happy and serene for the rest of your life," he said, and he knew he meant every word of it.

"That would mean you would suffer alone while I'm happy. I don't want that. We are to be one. Don't shut me out. Please."

He smiled. How did he become so lucky to have a woman like Louisa?

"I'm afraid, Louisa," he whispered. "You are a good woman, and I don't want to fail you. I don't want my past hurt to reflect on you and hurt you. I'd hate myself if that happened. You don't deserve that from me."

Instead of pulling away, Louisa inched even closer to him. She smiled. "And what do you think I deserve?"

"Love, above all things." He took her hand in his. "You deserve love, a love that ... that surpasses any other."

Slowly, her hands touched his cheeks. She shook her head, tears in her eyes. "No. I deserve you, William. Your love, your happiness, your sadness. I want everything."

He reached out to wipe away the tears that threatened to spill, his heart beating rapidly.

"You want everything?"

"Yes, William."

"Well, I am afraid because I'm still haunted by my past," he said, his voice low. "I'm a strong man, but when it comes to what happened all those years ago, I'm not so strong."

"You don't always have to be strong when you're with me, William. I will cherish all of you."

"But ... they died, Louisa." He ran a hand through his hair. "They died and I couldn't protect them. If ... if anything happens to you and I am not able to do anything, I won't forgive myself. I ..." He sighed. "I don't ever want to lose you."

"You won't lose me."

"How can you know that for sure?"

"Because I am here, with you, William." She smiled. "We will overcome this together. I promise you."

His hands itched and he pulled her to his chest, wrapping his arms around her petite frame. "You're a dream come true, Louisa."

The ache in his heart settled and it was all Louisa.

"Oh, I know. That's why you proposed, William," she teased, her arms wrapped tight around his back as well. "You offered me a future. A home. Do you regret it now?" she asked playfully.

William looked at her incredulously. "What? No! I don't regret it at all. Instead, I'm wondering why I didn't propose earlier. I hated seeing you dancing in the arms of another man."

She laughed, and it was the best music in the world. Then she looked at him seriously.

"Do you feel anything for me, William, or did you propose to me just because you couldn't stand to see me with another man?"

William took her hand and pressed it against his chest, where his heartbeat confessed his love for her over and over.

"What do you think, Louisa?"

She grinned and shrugged. "I wouldn't know. I'm not a mind reader."

"I feel a great deal for you, my dear Louisa," he confessed. "You're all I can feel."

Her grin widened and pink colored her cheeks.

"If that is so, then we shall face this together," she said softly, her eyes filled with love and understanding. "I won't let you face your fears alone."

Her words washed over him like a wave of comfort, and for the first time in a long while, he felt a glimmer of hope.

He hugged her tighter.

"Thank you, Louisa," he murmured, his voice choked with emotion. "For being here. For believing in me."

She smiled, her eyes sparkling in the moonlight. "Always, William. Always."

And as they stood there together, bathed in the moon's gentle glow, William felt a sense of peace wash over him.

Chapter 21: Louisa

A triumphant smile played on Louisa's lips as she exited the tiny, stone chapel, hand tucked firmly in William's arm.

The ceremony had been a whirlwind, and it had been brief as William requested.

No extravagant gowns, no overflowing guest lists. Just a handful of witnesses and the solemn pronouncement of their vows.

Although the white silk gown she picked out was very beautiful and she loved it, it was hardly the grand entrance into matrimony Louisa had envisioned. But none of that mattered.

Today, she was William's wife, and the gleam of gold on her finger—a simple band engraved with their initials—outshone any lack of pomp.

Sunlight filtered through the canopy of ancient oaks, casting dappled shadows on the cobblestone path leading from the chapel. The air was filled with the joyous chatter of their small group of friends and family, laughter mingling with the soft melodies of a string quartet.

As they descended the steps, a smattering of well-wishers—mostly locals who'd known William since childhood—offered their congratulations.

Amidst the throng of well-wishers, William and Louisa stood, their hands clasped tightly and their faces radiant with newlywed bliss.

Louisa's white gown seemed to glow in the afternoon light, complementing the vibrant bouquet she carried. She moved gracefully through the crowd, her laughter as infectious as the summer sun. William, ever the stoic, was transformed by a warmth that emanated from within. His eyes, usually guarded, held a tender affection as he gazed at her.

The Dowager Countess Blackwood stood apart from the main group. Her demeanor had softened somewhat, though her sharp blue eyes missed nothing.

As the newlyweds approached, she offered a warm smile, her voice carrying a hint of emotion. "My dearest William. My darling Louisa," she began, her tone filled with pride and affection. "To see you united in such happiness is a dream come true."

Louisa, taken aback by the countess's warmth, replied with heartfelt gratitude, "Thank you, Dowager Countess. Your blessing means more to us than you know."

The countess's eyes softened as she took Louisa's hands in hers. "You have brought such joy into William's life. I pray that your love will continue to grow stronger with each passing year. May your days be filled with laughter, your hearts with warmth, and your home with love."

As the countess released Louisa's hands, she turned to William. "My son," she said, her voice thick with emotion, "I have watched you grow from a boy into the remarkable man you are today. To see you standing here as a husband fills me with indescribable pride. Cherish her, William. She is a treasure beyond measure."

A big smile graced William's face as he embraced his mother, his gratitude evident in the silent strength of his hug. Louisa, moved by the heartfelt exchange, joined the embrace, feeling a profound connection to the woman who had raised the man she loved.

As the guests moved forward to offer their congratulations, the dowager countess watched the young couple with pride and contentment. With that, she turned and swept away, her dress billowing behind her.

As they walked to the waiting carriage, Louisa saw William was deep in thought.

"Penny for your thoughts, my dearest husband?" she teased, her voice laced with a playful challenge.

He blinked, a flicker of warmth in his eyes. "Simply pondering the journey ahead, my love," he replied, his voice a touch strained.

Louisa smiled widely, ready to tease him. "Journey? It's a short ride back to the estate. Surely you haven't grown weary of my company already?"

He gave a chuckle. "Never, Louisa. I just can't keep the excitement in."

Louisa, also not being able to contain her excitement, giggled and leaned closer to him. "I feel the same way. Can you believe it, William?" she exclaimed, her eyes sparkling with delight. "We're married!"

William's grin mirrored her own, his eyes alight with love. "I still can't quite believe it," he admitted, his voice filled with awe. "But I couldn't be happier, my love."

They boarded the waiting carriage, a handsome black coach emblazoned with the family crest. Inside, the plush leather seats and thick velvet curtains provided a welcome respite from the bright afternoon sun.

As they settled into the carriage, Louisa leaned into William's embrace, her heart overflowing with love. "I love you, William," she whispered, her voice tinged with emotion.

"I love you too, Louisa," William murmured, pressing a tender kiss to her forehead. "With all my heart."

As the carriage rolled smoothly along the country lane, the outside world faded away for William and Louisa.

The gentle sway of the vehicle and the rhythmic clip-clop of the horses' hooves created a soothing lullaby, and the couple found themselves lost in a bubble of their own.

They laughed and whispered sweet nothings, savoring every moment of their first journey together as husband and wife.

Louisa, the storyteller, began to regale William with tales of her life at the bookshop.

She painted vivid pictures of her days working with Mr. Abernathy at the bookshop, her voice filled with a nostalgic warmth. The eccentric patrons, the dusty shelves filled with forgotten worlds, the quiet solitude of the shop ... she brought it all to life for William.

He listened intently, eyes sparkling with amusement as she described the peculiar characters who frequented the shop.

Louisa snuggled closer to William, her head resting on his shoulder. "There was this curious gentleman who came into the bookshop asking for a book on alchemy." She giggled. "He looked so earnest, yet his eyes held a certain wildness."

William chuckled, a fond smile playing on his lips. "I remember a time I visited to speak with Abernathy, and there was a woman who insisted on borrowing a cookery book but spent the entire time discussing the intricacies of stargazing."

They shared a moment of laughter, their eyes sparkling with mirth.

Louisa continued, "Ah yes ... that was an adventure. And could I forget the young man who came in every day to read poetry aloud to himself? I half expected him to burst into verse at any moment."

William squeezed her hand. "Ah, the eccentric patrons of Mr. Abernathy's. A constant source of amusement. I'm happy it brought you such joy."

A comfortable silence fell between them as they gazed out the carriage window. The countryside was a patchwork of green fields and golden wheat, with the occasional farmhouse nestled amidst the landscape.

"Do you remember the day I went with you to a play?" Louisa asked, her voice soft.

William's eyes softened. "How could I forget? It was there that I first realized how truly special you are."

He pressed a kiss on the top of her head and she melted into his arm, the warmth of their love enveloping them like a soft blanket.

As the carriage continued its journey, the setting sun cast long shadows across the fields, painting the sky in hues of pink and gold. Inside the carriage, the world was a simpler place, filled only with the love shared by husband and wife.

As dusk settled, casting long shadows across the rolling hills, the carriage drew to a halt before the Blackwood estate.

Happiness washed over Louisa.

William helped her out of the carriage, his touch sweet, kind, and polite.

Inside, the estate was cozy, with a warm fire crackling in the hearth and the inviting scent of freshly baked bread in the air. A portly housekeeper greeted them with a generous smile and the promise of a hearty meal.

Louisa found herself drawn to the crackling fire. William joined her.

As they sat together, basking in the glow of their love, Louisa couldn't help but feel a deep sense of gratitude. She was married to the man of her dreams, her soulmate, her best friend. And in that moment, she knew that their love would only continue to grow stronger with each passing day.

With a contented sigh, she leaned into William's embrace, his arms wrapping around her protectively. In that moment, surrounded by love and warmth, Louisa knew that she was exactly where she was meant to be—in William's arms, for eternity.

Dinner was a lavish affair, a feast prepared with care by the estate's seasoned staff. The table was adorned with fine china, silver, and crystal, and the air was filled with the tantalizing scents of roasted meats, fresh vegetables, and buttery pastries. As they dined, their laughter echoed through the grand dining hall, a testament to the joy that filled their hearts.

The servants, accustomed to the earl's reserved demeanor, exchanged amused glances as they witnessed the couple's unabashed affection. William, ever the gentleman, carved the meat with ease, but his eyes never left Louisa's face. She, in turn, beamed with pride and adoration, her laughter a contagious melody that filled the room.

The evening wore on, and as the dessert course was cleared, the couple retired to the intimate drawing room. The fire crackled invitingly, casting dancing shadows on the walls. A bottle of fine wine was opened, and they toasted to their new life together.

Conversation flowed easily between them, ranging from the events of the day to their hopes and dreams for the future. Louisa, eyes sparkling with excitement, spoke of her desire to transform the estate's gardens into a haven of beauty and tranquility. William listened attentively, his hand finding hers beneath the low table.

"Whatever you wish, my love," he replied, his voice filled with tenderness. "The estate is yours as much as it is mine."

A comfortable silence fell between them as they shared a tender gaze. The world outside seemed to fade away, leaving only the two of them in their own private universe. As the fire began to dwindle, they moved closer, their bodies warming each other in the cool evening air.

With a gentle touch, William cupped Louisa's face, his thumb tracing the outline of her lips. She closed her eyes, savoring the moment, her heart filled with a love so profound it seemed to transcend the physical world.

"My dearest wife," he began, his voice low and husky, "this day has been more perfect than I could have ever imagined."

Louisa smiled, her heart full. "Mine too, William. Mine too."

He took her hand, gently pulling her closer. As their lips met in a soft, lingering kiss, the world seemed to fade away, leaving only the two of them in their own private paradise.

Louisa knew that in the days to follow, the newlyweds would settle into a rhythm of domestic bliss.

They would explore the sprawling estate, discovering hidden gardens and secluded groves. They would spend lazy afternoons curled up in the library, sharing books and dreams. And in the evenings, they would retire to their bedroom, their love a warm and comforting presence.

The estate staff would watch with a mixture of amusement and affection as the earl and countess blossomed in their new roles.

The stern, reserved earl would transform into a doting husband, and the spirited Louisa would have found a home filled with warmth and love.

She looked forward to those days.

Chapter 22: William

Flickering candlelight cast dancing shadows across the grand dining room, amplifying the silence that hung between William and Louisa.

It was a week after their wedding, and William still couldn't think of anything but the sight of his wife.

His wife.

The words made him smile and feel like a young man experiencing first love.

Marrying Louisa was the best decision of his life.

Meeting her at that ballroom had been the best gift the world had given him.

He stole a glance at her across the mahogany expanse of the table. She wore a simple emerald gown that shimmered with life, but she looked regal in it.

He thought back to the day they had wed. Each stolen glance, each brush of hands during the ceremony, had sent a jolt of longing through him. Throughout the day, conversation had been an exciting affair.

He'd wanted to keep hearing her soft soothing voice, to feel her fingers on his arm as she laughed or playfully smacked him when he said something mischievous.

William smiled to himself. He knew neither of them would forget that day for a very long time.

He was about to return to his food when, with a click of her fork against the china plate, Louisa looked up.

"Is this to be the standard operating procedure for our marriage, William?" she asked, waving her hands across the huge table.

William frowned. "What do you mean?"

"Do you not think we are too far apart?" she scoffed.

"Ah." He realized what she meant. "Now that you mention it, indeed we are." He shook his head. "This is how I was brought up, so I didn't think anything of it."

Louisa scrunched up her nose. "A tight-knit family is tight-knit in every situation."

"Even at the dining table?"

"Yes. Even here."

William chuckled. "Why, Louisa. I think you just want to be close to me."

She laughed. "You're right."

Silence.

"Well, will you not do anything about it?" she asked.

He dropped his fork and stretched his hand out to her.

"Come to me, wife."

A hot red rose up her cheeks as she slowly stood and walked over to him.

As she moved to sit on the chair next to him, his hand swept out, grabbed her wrist, and pulled her into his lap.

"William!" she exclaimed.

"Yes, dear wife?"

She giggled, wrapping her arms around his neck. "This was not what I meant by a tight-knit family!"

"Really?"

"Really."

"Well, I find that I quite like this position, wife."

Her blush deepened. "You're being naughty."

"Can I not?"

"Well, of course you can." Her eyes sparkled. "When shall we retire?"

He laughed. "My dear kitten, I don't think you're ready for such matters."

Her eyebrows furrowed. "I'm not ready?"

"Yes."

She scoffed. "What then? What do we do on a night like this?"

"Who says a husband's duty is performed only within the confines of the bedroom?"

Louisa leaned back against him. "And what ... duties," she drawled, emphasizing the word, "does this husband of mine plan to fulfill outside the bedroom, then?"

He chuckled, the sound warm and genuine, for the millionth time that day. "Perhaps," he countered, leaning forward conspiratorially, "he might regale his wife with tales of daring exploits in the world of cocoa bean trade."

A giddy smile touched Louisa's lips. "Oh wow. Cocoa bean exploits," she echoed, amusement dancing in her emerald eyes. "Sounds riveting, dear husband," she said, doing nothing to mask her sarcasm.

"Very," he said, adding a lightness to his voice.

She glared at him. "Do not make fun of me, dear husband."

"Alright, dear wife," he said, his lips stretching into a teasing grin. "Shall we retire then?"

She frowned. "You said I wasn't ready."

"I was making fun of you."

He snatched her up and raced up the stairs with the sound of her laughter booming in the estate.

Chapter 23: Louisa

A sliver of sunlight snuck through the heavy velvet drapes, dappling Louisa's face with soft warmth.

She stretched woozily, the luxurious sheets of her new bed a decadent contrast to the simple cot she'd known most of her life.

"Being the Countess of Havenwood isn't at all bad," she said to herself with a smirk.

The arrival to her duties had been a whirlwind.

The sprawling estate dwarfed her wildest dreams, with its manicured gardens, labyrinthine corridors, and a seemingly endless staff of dedicated servants.

Louisa, ever the pragmatist, had taken it all in stride.

Her first morning had been a sensory overload. A team of giggling maids, led by a formidable yet surprisingly warm woman named Agnes, had descended upon her.

They had fussed over her toilette, adorning her in a sumptuous silk gown the color of a summer sky. The gown, Agnes informed her with a conspiratorial wink, had been "specially chosen for the earl's eyes, my lady."

Louisa loved all of it and loved how considerate they were even more.

William had been the best, and she couldn't be happier. It all still felt like a dream to her.

This grand house, with its air of history and hushed whispers of past lives, held a certain allure, and Louisa was determined to explore every nook and cranny.

Her new lady's maid became an unexpected confidante. Agnes, with her sharp wit and unfaltering loyalty, was a breath of fresh air amidst the formality of the manor.

Life at Havenwood was an education in itself.

Days were filled with surprises: a troupe of acrobats performing on the manicured lawns, a whimsical tea party hosted by the head gardener amongst the blooming roses, and a seemingly endless stream of visitors seeking the earl's counsel.

Louisa, a natural social butterfly, relished the attention, charming the local gentry with her vivacious spirit and sharp wit. The villagers, initially wary of their new countess, were slowly warming to her down-to-earth demeanor. They delighted in her visits to their cottages, her genuine interest in their lives a stark contrast to the haughty indifference they were accustomed to from the nobility.

Today, however, Louisa craved solitude. She yearned to lose herself in the pages of a good book, a luxury she had long forgotten the feel of.

She instructed Agnes to saddle her mare, a fiery chestnut named Ember with a spirit as bold as her own.

The morning air was crisp and invigorating as Louisa, dressed in a simple yet elegant riding habit, looked up at the weather, the sun warming her back. Her destination: Mr. Abernathy's bookshop.

She found Agnes bustling about the stables.

"Oh, I heard about Mr. Abernathy's last weekend, Your Ladyship," Agnes chattered, her voice a constant stream of news and updates. "I heard he just received a new shipment from London, you know. Hear tell there's a travelogue about faraway lands with pictures as vivid as life itself!"

Louisa smiled, a welcome distraction from the constant whirlwind within the manor. "Then I must see it for myself, Agnes. Perhaps it will inspire another adventure for Ember and me."

Agnes clucked her tongue playfully. "Ember is a spirited creature, that's for sure. Just like you, Your Ladyship. Reminds me of my younger sister, bless her heart. Just had a bouncing baby boy last week, the little rascal."

A pang of longing tugged at Louisa's heart. Her own sister, Hannah, was miles away. News of her marriage to Duke Danvers had traveled all the way to London and to them here in Havenwood, a brief mention in the society pages that Louisa devoured with a mixture of joy and worry.

Had Hannah found happiness? Was her life filled with laughter and love, or was it a gilded cage like the one she'd feared for herself?

Pushing the thoughts aside, Louisa focused on the present. Agnes, ever observant, noticed the fleeting sadness that clouded her eyes.

"Thinking of something, Your Ladyship?" she inquired gently.

Louisa nodded. "My sister, Hannah. I hope she's well."

"She'll be just fine. Mark my words," Agnes declared, her voice laced with unwavering confidence. "Now, let's get you on that fiery mare of yours before the day gets any older. Mr. Abernathy's shelves won't explore themselves!"

With a renewed sense of purpose, Louisa allowed Agnes to help her mount Ember.

Riding through the picturesque countryside, Louisa felt a sense of freedom and joy. The worries and cares of the world melted away, replaced by profound peace and contentment. She reveled in the beauty of nature, the wind in her hair, and the sun on her face, feeling more alive than she had in years.

But, as she arrived at the village square, a sudden wave of dizziness overcame her, causing her to sway in the saddle. Her heart pounded in her ears, a frantic rhythm that seemed to echo the alarm bells ringing in her mind. Gripping the reins tightly, she forced herself to slow Ember's pace, her vision blurring at the edges.

A cold sweat broke out on her brow as the world around her seemed to tilt and spin. Fear, sharp and cold, clawed at her insides. Desperately, she sought a stable point, her gaze landing on the cobblestone street below. With a surge of adrenaline, she dismounted, her legs trembling as she touched the ground.

Leaning against Ember's warm flank, she closed her eyes, willing the dizziness to subside. The world seemed to be spinning out of control, and for a terrifying moment, she feared she might lose consciousness.

With determined effort, she opened her eyes and took a deep, slow breath. The world was still spinning, but the intensity had lessened. She was alone in the square, the villagers absorbed in their own affairs, oblivious to her distress.

Gathering her strength, she reached out to pat Ember's neck. "It's alright, girl. We're okay," she said, her voice a hoarse whisper.

The mare seemed to sense her rider's distress and nuzzled her hand gently. With renewed determination, Louisa attempted to climb back into the saddle.

As she tried to mount, another wave of dizziness washed over her. The world tilted on its axis, and the vibrant colors of the village square bled into a blurry mess.

Louisa gasped, her hand instinctively reaching out for support, but there was nothing to hold onto. The last thing she registered before succumbing to darkness was a panicked cry echoing in the air.

**

The world came back in fragments. A throbbing sensation behind her eyes, the faint scent of lavender, and the sound of a low, worried voice murmuring her name.

Blinking her eyes open, Louisa found herself nestled in a large, comfortable bed, white linen sheets framing her face. Agnes, her face tight with concern, hovered over her, gently pressing a cool compress on her forehead.

"My Lady," Agnes whispered, her voice trembling. "Thank goodness you're awake! We were so worried when word got to us that you fainted in the square."

Louisa winced at the memory. Faint? How utterly undignified.

"Fainted?" she repeated, her voice raspy. "What on earth brought that on?"

The memory of her fainting spell already fading from her mind, Louisa managed a smile.

She felt a surge of gratitude for Agnes and the others who had come to her aid, their kindness, and compassion a warm balm to her soul.

Agnes fussed over her, tucking the covers tighter. "The doctor says it's exhaustion, My Lady. You've been pushing yourself too hard these past few weeks."

Exhaustion? Louisa scoffed, the sound weak and brittle.

Adjusting to life in this sprawling manor, navigating the intricacies of her new role, the constant parade of unfamiliar faces—it was hardly arduous.

"Where... where is he? The earl?" she asked, her voice barely a whisper.

Agnes' face lit up. "He is on his way, my lady. I sent word to Mr. Abernathy already, and he will be sure to pass it on."

A smile spread on her face.

"Thank you, Agnes." Her joy was evident in her voice.

She was eager to see her husband.

The doctor bustled in then, a portly man with a booming voice and a cheerful demeanor that seemed grating in the face of her distress. He bustled around her, a whirlwind of forced joviality and unnecessary pronouncements.

"Nothing serious, Your Ladyship," he declared, his voice booming through the room. "Just a touch of fatigue. You need plenty of rest and some nourishing broth."

Louisa stared at him, her vision blurring with another wave of fatigue. 'Nothing serious,' he had said. She believed him. Now, she needed to see the love of her life.

She nodded and closed her eyes, shutting out everyone.

Could it really be nothing? She felt extremely weak.

She opened her eyes and looked at the doctor. "Doctor," she said, her voice barely a whisper, "tell me the truth. Is it exhaustion, truly? Or is there something else?"

The doctor, his jovial demeanor momentarily faltering, exchanged a quick, worried glance with Agnes.

He cleared his throat, his booming voice now oddly subdued. "Now, now, Countess," he soothed, "there's no need to fret. As I said, it's just a touch of fatigue—a common ailment easily remedied with rest and a healthy diet."

"Rest," Louisa echoed, skeptical.

She understood she needed rest, but what could be the cause of it? Horse riding?

Was that too much for her?

"But what caused this fatigue?" she pressed, her voice gaining a hint of its usual steel. "Surely, a healthy young woman doesn't simply faint out of the blue, Doctor."

The doctor shuffled his feet, his gaze flitting around the room as if searching for an escape route. "Well, stress, perhaps," he mumbled, his voice lacking conviction. "Adjusting to a new environment can be taxing on the body."

That makes sense, Louisa thought.

"Very well. Thank you," she said, her voice low. "If that's all, you may leave. "

The doctor, with a polite nod and smile, left the room.

"Please, Agnes," Louisa said, "let me know when the earl arrives."

Agnes nodded silently, her hand lingering on Louisa's before she retreated, leaving Louisa to rest.

Relieved that it was nothing serious, Louisa sank back into her pillows, allowing herself to relax and let go of her worries. She was safe and surrounded by people who cared for her, and that was all that mattered. The weight of concern seemed to lift from her shoulders, replaced by a gentle sense of peace.

As the day stretched on, Louisa drifted in and out of sleep, her dreams filled with visions of happiness and love. William's face, a beacon of warmth and comfort, appeared in her slumber, his smile a soothing balm to her weary mind. She dreamt of their wedding day, the vows they exchanged, the shared laughter, and the promise of a lifetime together.

As the sun dipped below the horizon, casting a warm glow over the room, Louisa closed her eyes and let herself drift into peaceful slumber. The gentle rhythm of her breath filled the quiet chamber, a testament to the tranquility that had finally enveloped her.

Chapter 24: William

William alighted from the carriage and walked toward his bookstore. His meeting with Monsieur Rosseau had been as tedious as he had anticipated, and now he just longed for the peace his bookstore always provided.

As he neared the entrance, his face morphed into a frown.

The door stood ajar.

Before he could cross the threshold, a frantic cry pierced the air. Mr. Abernathy, his usually composed face etched with worry, rushed from the store, his gait unsteady.

"My Lord!" he cried, his voice thick with panic. "Thank God you're here!"

A jolt of apprehension shot through William. The man's normally stoic demeanor, now shattered by worry, sent a tremor of fear down his spine. "What's wrong?"

Mr. Abernathy's face crumpled, and a tear escaped, tracing a glistening path down his weathered cheek. "Lady Louisa, sir," he stammered, his voice choked with emotion. "Agnes sent word some minutes ago. She fainted in the square. Suddenly, without warning. Someone called for a doctor, and Louisa was whisked away in a carriage."

The world seemed to tilt on its axis. Faint? Louisa?

A cold dread gripped his heart, a vice tightening around his lungs. Visions of her face, so full of life and happiness only yesterday, flashed before his eyes.

His heart threatened to burst as it felt like history was repeating itself all over again. "Where?" he rasped, his voice barely a whisper. "Where did they take her?"

Mr. Abernathy, bless his frantic soul, pointed a shaky finger down the cobbled street. "Back to the estate, My Lord."

Without another word, William tore off, his legs propelled by a raw, primal fear. The carriage—the safe, civilized mode of transportation—was suddenly an unbearable constraint.

He needed to get to Louisa, to see her with his own eyes, to feel the warmth of her hand in his and know that she was alright.

He didn't care about the curious stares of passersby, or the bewildered gasps at his frantic dash. His only focus was Louisa, the woman he loved, the woman he could never let go. The sunshine of his entire world.

Every cobblestone felt like a hurdle, every street corner a cruel delay. His lungs burned with exertion, but he couldn't stop—wouldn't stop—until he reached her side.

Regret, a bitter tide, washed over him. He should have stayed with her. He should have been there with his wife.

But now, as he raced through the bustling streets, he could only wish it was not too late. He needed to know that his wife was okay and nothing would happen to her, or he wouldn't survive it.

A strangled cry escaped his lips as he finally arrived at his home.

The doctor's carriage stood empty just by the huge gates, the door ajar like a mocking grin.

He burst through the doorway, his entire world shrunk to the need to find Louisa, to hear her voice, to feel her touch.

"Where is my wife?" he asked a maid scurrying past him.

"My Lord, she is in her chamber," the maid answered. "Luckily, the doctor was found, and he attended to her."

The relief that flooded him was mingled with a sickening dread.

What happened before? What had caused it?

He rushed to her chamber, only to find a man standing by the door. "My Lord." He bowed.

He was the doctor.

"How is my wife? Can I see her?"

The doctor nodded, his gaze lingering on William for a fleeting moment. "Of course, My Lord. But please, keep your visit brief. She needs her rest."

William followed the doctor back into Louisa's chamber, his heart pounding a frantic rhythm against his ribs.

Please, let her be alright. Please.

He couldn't lose her. He wouldn't lose her. Not now, not ever.

There, on her comfortably padded bedding, lay Louisa. Her usually vibrant face was pale, a tear glistening on her cheek like a single pearl. The sight of her distress sent a jolt through him, a raw mixture of fear and a desperate, aching need to comfort her.

In a single stride, he was at her bedside, his heart hammering like a trapped bird in his chest.

He reached out, a tremor running through his hand as he brushed a strand of hair from her damp forehead. The contact, however faint, seemed to anchor him, grounding him in the face of an unknown storm.

"Louisa," he rasped, his voice thick with emotion. "What happened? Are you alright?"

She looked up at him, her eyes red-rimmed and filled with a vulnerability that ripped at his core. A single sob escaped her lips, and his own composure shattered. Tears welled up in his eyes, blurring her already blurry form.

"William," she choked out, her voice barely a whisper. "You're here. I was so afraid."

He sank to his knees beside the bed, burying his face in her hand, the warmth of her touch a balm to his raw emotions.

"I should have been here. I should have been here with you," he muttered. "Forgive me. I love you, Louisa. More than words can express. I can't ever lose you."

"William," she breathed, her trembling hand reaching up to cup his cheek. "It's not your fault. You had your meeting. Don't blame yourself for this."

"But—"

"No buts. See? I'm alright. I'm fine and here with you, and I love you so much."

He pulled back, his tear-filled gaze meeting hers.

"I love you, Louisa. You can't ever leave me."

A tear escaped the corner of her eye, and a smile, fragile yet beautiful, bloomed on her pale lips. "I won't."

And then, just as their foreheads touched, the door creaked open, shattering the intimate moment.

The doctor, his face a mask of professional neutrality, appeared in the doorway. William reluctantly pulled back, a silent apology hanging in the air.

"My Lord," the doctor said.

William understood. He turned to Louisa and caressed her cheek. "Get some rest, my love," he said. "I'll be right outside. I'm not leaving you alone again."

"Thank you, dear husband,' Louisa said, her voice weak, "but you need some rest yourself."

He started to protest, but she shook her head at him.

"Go." She smiled up at him. "I'll be fine."

He returned her smile. "Alright, dear wife."

With that, he turned and exited the room. He felt lighter knowing that she was alright, but he made a silent promise to himself to never be far from her again.

Chapter 25: Louisa

A shaft of golden sunlight slanted through the window of the charming library William had built for her, illuminating the pages of the newspaper spread across her lap.

A satisfied smile curved Louisa's lips as she read the headline: "Lord Thorne and Lady Beatrice Apprehended in Daring Raid! Hastings Estate Returned to Rightful Heir."

Justice, it seemed, had finally served its course.

The wicked had been vanquished, their web of deceit exposed. The Hastings Estate, rightfully hers, would be a new chapter, a chance to forge a brighter future.

A light rap on the door drew her attention.

"Come in, Agnes," she called, her voice laced with contentment.

The door creaked open, and Agnes, her face beaming, bustled in with a steaming cup of tea.

Louisa chuckled, accepting the cup with a grateful smile. "Ah. Raspberry leaf tea. Just what the doctor ordered."

The scent of berries filled the air, a comforting reminder of the life growing within her.

Months had passed since her fainting episode, and the truth, later revealed by the doctor, had filled her with both joy and apprehension. She was carrying William's child, a tiny miracle blossoming within her.

"Your guests will be arriving soon, My Lady," Agnes announced, her voice hushed with excitement.

Louisa's heart swelled.

Two months ago, upon receiving a letter from Hannah detailing the birth of her son, Louisa had extended an invitation. The prospect of having her sister under her roof, a chance to rebuild their fractured bond, filled her with an anticipation that rivaled the excitement of motherhood.

"Splendid," Louisa declared, taking a sip of the calming tea. "Where is William?"

"In his study, My Lady," Agnes replied. "Busy with some estate matters, I believe."

A contented sigh escaped Louisa's lips.

She had a playful glint in her eyes. Perhaps a little teasing was in order.

Placing the teacup on a nearby table, she announced, rising to her feet, "Well, I suppose I ought to go check on my husband. Wouldn't want him to be too busy with his paperwork to see his wife, would we?"

Agnes chuckled, her eyes twinkling. "Indeed, my lady. Though, I daresay the earl would find a way to neglect even the most pressing matters if it meant spending time with you."

Their conversation was interrupted by a new voice that boomed from the doorway. "Speaking of seeing one's wife," it declared, laced with amusement.

Agnes excused herself, and Louisa turned to find William leaning against the doorframe, a broad grin on his face.

He crossed the room in a few quick strides, a look that Louisa knew all too well in his eyes. Before she could react, he swept her off her feet, holding her close in a warm embrace.

A surprised squeal escaped her lips, followed by a fit of giggles. The world tilted momentarily, then righted itself as William spun her around, his laughter echoing in the small library.

"William!" she squealed, a mixture of amusement and mild panic blooming in her voice. "Put me down at once!"

He chuckled, the sound like warm honey against her ear. "Not until you admit how much you missed me, my love." He showered her cheeks with light kisses, his breath tickling her skin.

"Missed you?" Louisa scoffed, feigning annoyance. "The library and Agnes' delightful company have been more than enough entertainment, thank you very much."

William's eyes crinkled at the corners. "Indeed? Then perhaps I should relinquish my role as your sole source of amusement."

Louisa swatted playfully at his arm, her laughter bubbling up. "Don't be ridiculous," she chided, a smile softening her features.

He finally deposited her back on her feet, his hands lingering possessively on her waist.

"My apologies, my love," he murmured, his voice husky with emotion. "I couldn't resist. You looked utterly captivating bathed in the sunlight."

Louisa blushed, a warmth blooming in her cheeks. "Flattery will get you everywhere, Earl," she teased, her tone playful yet laced with affection.

William's gaze dropped to her midsection, a tenderness filling his eyes. "And how fares the little one?" he inquired softly.

The news of her pregnancy, initially a source of worry, had become a beacon of hope for their future. William's love and unwavering support had chased away her fears, replaced by a blooming excitement.

"Restless, just like its mother," she replied with a wink. "But the doctor assures me it's nothing but healthy activity."

William chuckled, his hand gently resting on her belly. "A little hellion, then?"

"Perhaps," Louisa agreed, her eyes mirroring his warmth. "Just like its father."

The sound of carriage wheels crunching on the gravel path outside drew their attention.

Agnes appeared at the doorway, her face beaming. "Your sister has arrived, my lady."

Louisa's heart swelled with joy. Hannah was here. With a shared look of anticipation, she and William walked hand-in-hand out of the library.

Stepping onto the front terrace, Louisa felt a wave of warmth wash over her. Laughter filled the air as Hannah, a radiant vision cradling a swaddled bundle, emerged from the carriage. Duke , ever the supportive husband, followed closely behind, a wide smile on his face.

Louisa's breath hitched. In Hannah's arms, nestled peacefully in a sea of white lace, slept a cherub-faced baby boy. A rush of maternal instinct filled her, a yearning to hold her own precious cargo that was still growing within.

"Hannah!" Louisa cried, her voice brimming with emotion.

Hannah's eyes met hers, a wave of recognition lighting up her face. With a joyful cry, she hurried towards the open arms waiting for her. The sisters locked in a tight embrace, tears of joy and relief mingling on their cheeks.

William reached them then, a warm smile on his lips. He extended a hand to Duke Dan, their greetings full of camaraderie.

The afternoon unfolded in a warm blur of laughter and shared stories. Louisa introduced Hannah to the wonders of her new library, while William proudly showed off their newly cultivated rose garden.

The baby, christened Thomas after their late father, became the star of the show, his wide, inquisitive eyes taking in his new surroundings with innocent wonder.

As the sun began its descent, painting the sky in hues of orange and pink, the two sisters found themselves nestled on a comfortable settee.

"I'm so happy for you, Louisa," Hannah whispered, her voice filled with genuine warmth. "You deserve all this happiness."

Louisa squeezed her sister's hand. "And you too, Hannah. Danvers seems like a wonderful man."

They sat in comfortable silence for a while, Thomas' soft coos filling the gaps within their conversation.

Louisa realized with a contented sigh that life wasn't always about grand balls and whispered gossip. True happiness resided in the quiet moments, the love and support of family, and the promise of a future filled with laughter and light.

As the first stars twinkled in the darkening sky, William and Duke Danvers joined them, their voices weaving a tapestry of plans for future visits.

Louisa looked around at the faces she loved, her heart brimming with gratitude that overflowed.

The trials they had faced had only served to strengthen their bonds, reminding them of the importance of family, forgiveness, and the enduring power of love.

This was the beginning of a new life filled with the promise of a richer, fuller, and more joyful life than any she could have ever dreamed.

THE END

Thank you for reading "Louisa, The Heiress In Disguise."

If you loved this book, you will love the first book in my Somersley Series Entitled "Governess Penelope and a Duke!"

It's a feel-good story about an unexpected second chance with a first love.

Click here and get your FREE copy of "Governess Penelope and a Duke": https://dl.bookfunnel.com/a5l15u9hpa

In 1811 London, Penelope, a governess disowned by her father, discovers love while preparing her friend's niece for society.

This full-length second-chance romance offers a happily-ever-after ending,

Click here and get your FREE copy of Governess Penelope and a Duke now! https://dl.bookfunnel.com/a5l15u9hpa

Please Leave a Review for "Louisa, The Heiress In Disguise." https://www.amazon.com/review/create-review?&asin=B0DFQH1MDH

Made in the USA
Monee, IL
01 October 2024